These are dangerous times...

Bolan crossed the seedy office, his eyes and gun never wavering from Benny Copa's pallid face.

"Easy, man," said Benny. "There must be some mistake."

"You made it, Benny."

"Well, hey. I mean...it can't be all that bad can it?"

Bolan's face and voice were hard. "That depends on you. You have some information and I want it. You give, you live. That simple."

"Well, hey," blurted Copa, "I know nothing. Honest."

"Goodbye, Benny," said Bolan. The Beretta slid out to full extension.

"Wait," yelped Benny. "Maybe we can make another deal...."

Bolan said nothing. Behind Benny's weasel eyes, he could see the gears clicking into place as Copa came to a belated realization.

"I know you—you're supposed to be *dead*." The hoodlum suddenly leered, his eyes greedy with the deal he wanted to make.

"So are you," Bolan told him.
And the Beretta chugged once.

About the author

Don Pendleton is a much decorated veteran of World War II who saw action in the North Atlantic U-boat wars, the invasion of North Africa, as well as the assaults on Iwo Jima and Okinawa. He was also among the very first Americans to land in Japan just before the surrender, and he later served in Korea. He has since worked in the missile and aerospace industries.

An author of wide experience, he has captivated millions of readers with the compelling drive and absolute credibility of his writing. In ten years, Don Pendleton's *Executioner* books have become bestsellers in many languages throughout the world. In Mack Bolan, Pendleton has created a classic modern hero big enough to take on the most powerful forces of crime and terrorism.

"Mack is not a mindless killer," says the author. "He is proclaiming that humanity is important, that it does matter what happens here, that universal goals are being shaped on this cosmic cinder called earth. Bolan is an American hero whose actions are fast and effective. I only wish the world had more men like him, leaders with commitment, principles, dedication and bravery—the so-called old-fashioned virtues that were so evident in 1776."

MACK

THE EXECUTIONER 41

BOLAN

The Violent Streets

DON PENDLETON

A GOLD EAGLE BOOK FROM
WORLDWIDE

TORONTO • LOS ANGELES • NEW YORK • LONDON • PARIS • SYDNEY

Published March 1982

First printing February 1982

ISBN 0-373-61041-6

Special thanks and acknowledgment from the author to
Mike Newton for his contributions to this work.

Printed in U.S.A.

"Freedom both for the individual and for the masses hangs above the abyss of tyranny by the thread of respect for others."

—Chen Ping Liau

"When savages own the streets, fear rules the city and our great cities are jungles once more. A truly civilized man cannot tolerate this. So where is your outrage? Where is your fury? The streets *can* be yours again."

—Mack Bolan, "The Executioner"

Dedicated to the more than 150 law—
enforcement men and women who give
their lives every year in defense against
the predators that inhabit our human
jungle.

PROLOGUE

The Bill of Rights was designed by men who were justly concerned about the role of government in the personal affairs of its citizens. Individual rights were thereafter closely delineated in the U.S. Constitution and enshrined as "the American way": a blueprint for life, liberty and the pursuit of happiness in a fair society.

Mack Bolan knew, however, that some Americans regarded this blueprint cynically and selfishly, as a "free ride," an avenue toward their own evil goals unhampered by official restraints—as a "picnic" where every lust is easily sated, every desire freely fulfilled. For many people—even, sadly, for some Americans—"freedom" means only that liberty found in jungle law.

From Bolan's journal: "These violent streets are not part of the America envisioned by Jefferson and his colleagues. Those men saw government as the largest potential threat to freedom. But how hollow is a freedom that cannot guarantee our wives and mothers and daughters freedom from sexual assault, that will not enforce the sanctity of the home and the protection of hard-earned property? What comfort, then, is freedom—on savagely violent streets? It's jungle comfort, John, and that's a hell of a bitter epitaph for the home of the brave."

The last line in that quote was directed at himself—in his new identity as John Phoenix, head of the government's covert-operations group. One may only guess at the line of thought that prompted that cryptic communiqué to the self. It was a line of thought born of the almost unbearable stresses of his personal campaign against the Mafia, a campaign itself born of his terrible years of war, and of his absence then from his homeland while the country endured stresses of its own— the stresses of great change and of renewed exposure to the predators of our jungle cities.

Mack Bolan, AKA John Phoenix, has been at war now for years, but freedom has not been secured. It would be foolish, insane, to imagine that it could be otherwise. But certain freedoms, certain inviolable rights of safety, should be possible and given at whatever the level of society, and when it is those very basic rights that are violated— and violated upon the person of Bolan's closest kin, or the kin of his closest friends and allies— then the war takes on new heat, new force, new dimensions of strength, resilience. . . and attack.

Mack Bolan returned from Turkey seriously exhausted by the demands of defending and maintaining personal freedom. But nothing, no possible restriction of body and mind, could halt him in his response to a plea from his friend Rosario Blancanales. It is in this response that the jungle predators meet their match and comfort is at last taken from the criminal and given back to its rightful recipient, the free citizen. Even Mack Bolan knows, as well as his enemies, that in these times there is absolutely no avoiding the Executioner.

1

The sleek Lear jet touched down lightly on the east-west runway of Holman Field in St. Paul. Wind-blown rain streaked the Plexiglas window beside the single passenger, turning the world outside the aircraft into a dark blur speckled with runway lights. Interior lighting reflected his frown in the oval pane.

They had approached from the east, descending through one of those Minnesota thunderstorms that always seem to reserve themselves for summer and then invariably strike around midnight. It was after midnight now, and the big man was anxious to be about his business in St. Paul.

The Lear's pilot taxied his craft to a slow halt near a western terminal. Holman Field sits tucked into a hairpin curve of the Mississippi River, where it bites a half-moon slice out of south-central St. Paul and Ramsey County. The compact jet's position placed it on the far side of the airfield, well away from the busier avenues occupied by commercial airliners and most private traffic.

Mack Bolan snared a heavy flight bag from the reclining seat beside him and moved out down the center aisle. His plainclothes Air Force pilot met

him at the exit port, throwing the door back on
its runners to admit a blast of wind and stinging
rain.

Somewhere across the looping river, lightning
blotched the sky, and was followed instantly by
the intestinal growl of distant thunder. Bolan nodded to the pilot, hunched his shoulders against the
storm, and descended folding steps into the rainy
darkness.

Beyond the concrete retaining wall, near a
vacant-looking terminal building, a long, dark
sedan sat with engine idling. Bolan took it in at a
glance and angled in that direction, slowing his
pace slightly in spite of the pouring rain.

As if on cue, the sedan's interior dome light was
turned on, revealing the driver's solemn, familiar
face, and was quickly extinguished. Bolan picked
up his pace, jogging now until he reached the
waiting car, and slid in on the passenger's side,
flight bag between his feet.

"How is she, Pol?" he asked the man behind the
wheel.

Rosario Blancanales shrugged listlessly. "She's
in bad shape, Mack. And emotionally...who
knows?" After brief hesitation, he added,
"Thanks for coming, Sarge."

"I'll pretend I didn't hear that, guy," Bolan told
him.

Blancanales put the sedan in motion, away
from the airport and onto Lafayette Freeway,
heading north to cross the wide Mississippi into
St. Paul proper. They spoke little as they drove,

each man occupied with private thoughts on that
stormy Minnesota night.

Mack Bolan was trying to remember when he
had last seen his old friend look so harried, so
drained. Not in Asia, certainly, where Rosario's
vitality and savvy with the natives had quickly
earned him the nickname "Politician." Nor later,
when Pol joined the Executioner's domestic war
against a common enemy. Not even at the bottom,
the very worst of it, after the massacre at Balboa
in the bad old days.

Bolan decided that his friend had never looked
worse, or had better cause.

Perhaps—just maybe—there was something he
could do to change all that.

Blancanales, meanwhile, for all the strain evident on his face and in his posture, seemed to
draw some sort of solace from the mere presence
of his best and oldest friend. Already he seemed
to be regaining a touch of the old fire, as if Bolan's
welcome arrival from his last mission in Turkey
had sparked some internal mechanism and set the
wheels turning again.

Bolan noted the subtle changes and was thank-
ful for it.

Holman Field was twenty minutes behind them
when Pol broke the silence with a clipped, curt
warning.

"We've got a tail," he snapped.

Bolan glanced back over his shoulder through
rain-streaked darkness.

"No question?"

Blancanales shook his head. "Negative. The last three turns were for his benefit. He's sticking tight."

A block behind them, headlights hung on their track at an even, measured pace. When Pol accelerated, the twin lights edged nearer; when he stroked the brake lightly, they fell back.

A tail, yeah. No question about that.

Bolan turned back to his friend in the driver's seat. "Okay, we'd better lose him."

"Roger that, buddy."

Pol instantly swung the sedan into a groaning turn, barely making the light and the corner as he swung across two lanes of traffic onto an intersecting street. The tail car never missed a beat, edging out two other vehicles as it slashed a course behind them in pursuit.

Blancanales was an expert wheelman, familiar with the streets and alleys of St. Paul. With Mack Bolan at his side, silently urging him on, he pulled out all the stops, using every trick to shake the tenacious pursuers dogging their tracks. Up and down one-way alleys, through red and amber lights, cutting corners across parking lots and filling stations. Nothing served to shake the dogged hunters.

Outside the car, the driving rain subsided to a drizzle, and the buildings rapidly transformed themselves from large commercial structures to small businesses, finally merging into dark and sleeping residential tracts. Pol's course took them north and east by stages, running serpentine, with the tail car close behind them all the way.

Two minutes into the winding chase, the pursuers gained speed and drew within two or three car lengths of Pol's speeding sedan. Dirty orange flame winked from the passenger side of the tail, followed by the hollow sound of a bullet striking the sedan's trunk lid. Bolan glanced backward in time to see a second muzzle flash, and this time the slug chipped window glass before whining off chrome and steel into darkness.

Bolan reached between his feet and opened the zippered flight bag. He hauled out an Ingram M-10 9mm machine pistol. He snapped a thirty-two-round magazine into the vertical pistol grip, then threaded a foot-long silencer onto the Ingram's squat muzzle.

The weapon was a man-shredder, conceived during the riot-torn sixties as a lethal "room broom" for use in sweeping snipers out of the urban combat zones. It was designed to fire those 9mm manglers at a rate of twelve hundred rounds per minute, but Bolan had modified and tamed this particular model down to a more economical—and manageable—seven hundred rpm's.

It was more than enough, yeah, in any situation under a hundred yards. And Bolan planned to confront his present foe much closer than that.

He snapped back the cocking bolt, bringing a cartridge into the chamber and priming the lethal little weapon. Pol Blancanales shot a quick glance at the hardware, shaking his head grimly as he recognized the chopper and its capabilities.

"Give me some stretch, Pol," the Executioner said.

"You've got it, man," his driver replied.

Blancanales stomped hard on the accelerator to wring another five miles an hour out of the laboring engine. Behind them in darkness, the trailing headlights lurched, then drew closer, gaining.

"I need a face-off," Bolan said softly. "Choose your own time."

Blancanales snapped his friend a curt nod, craning forward over the wheel, his eyes scanning the dim street from side to side. He saw his opening, in the form of a midnight-dark side street racing toward them on their right.

Bolan saw it coming too, reading the scene and his comrade's tense body language behind the wheel. Both men braced themselves.

"Okay, buddy," Pol grated over the roar of the engine, "right...about...*Now!*"

2

Pol cranked hard on the steering wheel of the sedan, working the accelerator and brake pedals expertly to put the car into a tire-smoking turn at the mouth of the darkened side street. The headlights revealed a short cul-de-sac lined with silent, sleeping houses.

Blancanales floored the accelerator, and the sedan leaped forward, aimed directly at the sloping front lawn of a large house dead ahead. Suddenly he slammed on the brakes and twisted the wheel hard to the left, rewarded by the scream of tortured rubber as the car slid into a 180-degree bootlegger's turn. Pol instantly killed the headlights, making the half-spin in sudden darkness.

Bolan was out of the car and crouching, the Ingram poised, before the sedan rocked to a complete halt. His combat senses were primed and alert, probing the hostile night.

In an instant the chase car roared into the cul-de-sac on two wheels, high-beam headlights knifing through blackness as the driver struggled to right his vehicle. For a split second the onrushing beams were blinding, then Pol Blancanales switched on his own lights, kicking them up into high beam and framing the hurtling attack car in the brilliant glare.

Bolan caught a brief glance of two hard-faced men inside, both bringing their arms up to shield their eyes against the sudden blinding light. The driver was hunched forward over the steering wheel, and the passenger on his right had an arm out the side window, his silencer-equipped pistol blindly seeking a target.

Bolan stroked the trigger of the Ingram, and the stubby machine pistol made a sound like canvas ripping. He tracked the flashing muzzle from left to right in a surgically precise twelve-round burst. A row of neat, even holes blossomed across the attack car's windshield, spider web cracks obscuring the suddenly terrified faces within.

Already dying, the driver tried to control his vehicle for another faltering heartbeat before he lost it all. Bolan helped him get there with another short burst to the driver's side, this time seeking flesh and finding it.

The windshield imploded, and at once the front wheels locked into a death slide, much too sharp, sending the big car into a wide, looping roll that ended with the vehicle upside down across the sidewalk, its nose amid the ruins of a white picket fence. One of the occupants was ejected during that wallowing roll, his rag doll body twisting and flopping across the pavement like a punctuation mark to the auto's emphatic death sentence.

There was little time to verify the hit. Already porch lights were coming on around the cul-de-sac, brightening the grim arena. The numbers were falling, fast.

But Bolan was willing to spend a few of those precious numbers, sure, to find a handle on this brief and lethal encounter. It would not do to quit the field of battle without some effort to identify the fallen enemy.

Bolan and the Politician crossed the street to stand above the limp, lifeless form. Bolan recognized the man as the passenger, out of character now as he lay on his back, one arm twisted awkwardly beneath him, his bloodied head cocked at an impossible angle. A dark ribbon of blood dripped from one ear, staining the asphalt.

"Do you make the face, Pol?" Bolan asked his comrade.

Blancanales shook his head firmly. "No. He's a stranger to me."

Bolan shot a swift glance toward the capsized auto, but another porch light clicked on just across the street, making the decision for him. Together, the surviving warriors trotted back to their vehicle and put that street of death behind them before sleepy residents could spill out onto lawns and sidewalks.

Pol tore out at speed, then slowed the sedan to a more sedate pace, avoiding the risk of a routine traffic stop by roving police. Beside him, in the passenger's seat, Bolan was dismantling the Ingram and stowing its warm components back inside the flight bag.

But the Executioner's mind was not on the

mechanical functions of stripping his weapon. No way. His brain was already in overdrive, racing toward analysis and recognition of the real game in St. Paul.

They were stopped at a traffic light when Pol's voice intruded on those dark thoughts.

"I guess I'll have to lose this heap," he grumbled. Then, with a rueful grin, he added, "Just like the bad old days, eh?"

Bolan frowned. "The old days are supposed to be dead and buried, guy."

Blancanales nodded, losing the grin. "So are you, buddy, so are you."

"How do you read this action, Pol?" Bolan asked, changing the subject.

Blancanales shrugged. His face in the dim dashboard light was genuinely puzzled.

"No reading, Sarge. Not yet, anyway. It just won't compute. It's beyond me."

For another few moments they drove along in silence, each warrior preoccupied with his own private thoughts and concerns. Each sought some personal answer, some private point of recognition in the puzzle that ensnared them.

Neither found it.

3

Long miles lay between the deadly poppy fields of
his recent mission in Turkey and the rainy streets
of St. Paul, Minnesota, but Mack Bolan, the man
now known as Colonel John Phoenix, had early
learned to take his hellgrounds and his enemies
where he found them. And that could be anywhere.

It was all one struggle, sure. All part of the
same universal conflict, and you didn't need a
program to tell the players apart if you could only
get a handle on the game.

There were, of course, no living losers in the
game.

Bolan had returned only hours earlier from the
Turkish hellground, anxious for a brief respite
from his war everlasting. The targets had been
opium and the men who grew it. The method: total
destruction. Executioner style.

And yes, Bolan had been more than happy to
find the brief sanctuary of his Phoenix base,
located on Stony Man Farm in the lovely Blue
Ridge mountain country of Virginia. He could find
peace there, or at least the illusion of peace.

But there would be no real peace at Stony Man

Farm for Mack Bolan. Not on this return trip from the universal hellground.

He had been welcomed home by April Rose and Aaron "The Bear" Kurtzman, warriors-in-residence at the Phoenix base. Behind the lovely young woman's kiss of greeting and her sparkling eyes, Bolan had read a message of concern, even distress.

Something, yeah, had been happening on the home front while Bolan was circling the eastern frontiers, stomping vipers.

The last of the telexes had been received forty-five minutes before Bolan's arrival by air. The Executioner spent the next forty-five in gentle, aimless conversation with April, unwinding from his recent brush with death. He spoke in the vague generalities of a man who hates to worry his woman, and she listened with the incisive knowledge of a woman who lives on the fine edge between exultation and despair.

For the moment, though, simple gratitude was enough for both of them.

They were both alive, yeah, and ready to fight another day against yet another enemy. On another hellground.

And every day above ground was a good day for Mack Bolan and his woman.

The expected telephone call had come exactly on schedule, and Aaron the Bear had fetched Bolan from his seat on the porch of Stony Man's ranch house. April had stayed behind, watching him go with sad, knowing eyes.

Pol Blancanales was on the line, his normally firm voice almost cracking, his words dripping with grateful relief.

"Mack...thank God...I was afraid...." He broke off, as if struggling to collect disordered thoughts before continuing.

"Easy, Pol," the Executioner said. "Give it to me one piece at a time, from the beginning."

Something caught in the Politician's throat, far away at the other end of the line.

"Jesus, Mack, it's Toni. I...I...."

He broke off again, but already he had said enough to raise Bolan's hackles, letting him know that there was something deadly personal about this cry for help.

Toni Blancanales was the Politician's kid sister. And some "kid," yeah. All woman, that kid, and no question about it.

During the Executioner's home-front Mafia wars, she had worked on occasion with Bolan and the members of Able Team, and since the birth of the Phoenix project, she had been handling the overt aspects of Able Team's ongoing private eye business.

Bolan had the highest respect and affection for her.

There had been some physical substance to that mutual affection once, lifetimes ago and far away, on yet another hellground. Bolan cherished the memory of that brief encounter and relegated it to the untouchable, unreclaimable past.

But he loved the lady, sure, in his way. And always would.

So the trouble was Toni in St. Paul. The kid sister.

"Take your time, Pol," Bolan had urged his distraught comrade-in-arms. "What about Toni?"

At the other end, Blancanales drew a deep, ragged breath before continuing.

"She's been beaten, Sarge. Beaten bad. And... and raped."

The last word came out as a strangled whisper, but it rang in Bolan's ear like the thunderous blast of close-range gunfire. Something turned over inside him.

He regained control swiftly. No observer would have seen it slip away from him. But his hand was white-knuckled as he gripped the telephone receiver.

"Is she going to be all right, Pol? Is she in the hospital?"

Blancanales hesitated. Then his voice was low and clipped. "She was, but I got her out of there. I couldn't leave her in there, Mack."

Bolan sensed something underneath his old friend's words, a tension beyond the fury of an outraged brother. "You'd better fill me in, Pol," he said.

"Jesus, Mack, I don't know where to start. Toni was already in the hospital when I got word about... about what happened. I went right over, and Jesus...."

Bolan waited for his friend to regain his composure and continue. Pol's voice came back at him almost as a whisper. Bolan could hear the guy choking on his pain as he spoke.

"I couldn't believe it when I saw her, Sarge. I mean, it looked like she'd been worked over by two or three guys, not just one..." He hesitated again, then forged ahead. "Hell, I've seen worse. We both have, hundreds of times. But it's different when it hits close to home. Very different."

And sure, the Executioner knew all about being hit close to home. Just such a blow to the heart had inspired his original "hopeless war," and the memories of martyred friends, the wounded and the dead, stretched out behind him like milestones on a personal road to hell. Mack Bolan had made the journey once, full circle, and he had returned to begin again.

Pol Blancanales was speaking to him, bringing Bolan back again to the here and now.

"You should have seen her," he was saying, "all stretched out up there in the ward, looking like death warmed over. I didn't recognize her at first. My own kid sister, for God's sake. They had her hooked up to an I.V., and bandages all over— Christ, I thought she was dying."

"What did the medics tell you?"

"Lots of nothing. Abrasions and contusions, a mild concussion—you know the routine, Sarge. She has hairline fractures on a couple of ribs, but no internal injuries, thank God. Three of her fingers were dislocated when she tried to protect herself. And then...of course, she was raped."

"You know it could have been worse," Bolan said.

"Yes, it could have been worse."

Mack Bolan realized that his friend was walking on the razor-edge of hysteria.

"Easy, Pol," he cautioned. "You've got to hold it together. For Toni."

"She could barely recognize me, Sarge," he said, swallowing. "They had her so doped up.... But when she made out who I was, she started crying, and she said she was ashamed—"

Bolan cut him off. "When did the doctors decide to release her?" he asked.

The question took Blancanales by surprise.

"Oh, they didn't. I just sort of checked her out on my own."

"How's that?"

"Well, goddammit, I couldn't leave her lying up there like a slab of meat on display. She was dying inside, Mack. And the place wasn't what I call secure. So I checked around, made sure the I.V. was only S.O.P. for shock instead of life-support. Then I bagged an orderly's uniform from the laundry room and picked up a wheelchair in the hallway. She was home in bed before those turkeys knew that she was gone."

"You were taking one hell of a chance, Pol."

"You know, I believe it would have been a much bigger chance leaving her there in the open," insisted Blancanales. "I have to check some things out, see what's out of line."

He paused. There was anguish in his voice.

"Listen, Sarge, something's wrong with this case. I mean...hell, I'm not sure what I mean, and I hate to say any more on an open line. Can you come?"

What in hell do you say to an old friend and fellow warrior when he tells you that his sister, a girl as close—closer—than your own, has been trapped and torn by animals?

You tell him that you'll do anything to help, go anywhere.

Kill anyone.

Sure, all of that. You owe it to him, and to her.

You owe it to yourself.

"I'm on my way," the Executioner told his friend without hesitation.

And the meeting had been set for Holman Field, just over two hours from Stony Man by light plane. Bolan allowed himself an extra hour for preparation, and scheduled the meeting for midnight. The gratitude and relief in the Politician's voice was full of pathos, almost more than Bolan could stand.

Can you come?

Rather, ask: Can you turn your back on a friend in torment?

No.

It was not within Mack Bolan's power to ignore that plea for help. Not if he could answer in the affirmative with the last breath of life.

The quality of caring and of empathy for the wounded and dying of the hellgrounds had earned Bolan the nickname "Sergeant Mercy" on the

Asian battlefields, even while his marksmanship and coolness under fire were winning him the "Executioner" label.

It took a big man to carry both names well.

And Mack Samuel Bolan was one hell of a big man.

4

After picking up a new rental car and ditching their riddled sedan on a lonely side street, Pol Blancanales and Mack Bolan drove directly to a fashionable apartment complex east of downtown St. Paul. They were not followed.

On their way up two flights of stairs, Pol filled Bolan in on some of the background to Toni's case. She had been living in St. Paul the past three months, working out of this same apartment building while handling some of Able Team's business that was unrelated to the covert Phoenix effort.

They reached a nondescript door on the third-floor front, and Pol gave a prearranged knock before letting himself in with his key. Mack Bolan followed his friend into a modest but comfortable living room, where the lights were kept on their lowest setting, casting shadows in the corners of the room.

Toni Blancanales was emerging from a rear bedroom to greet them, and Bolan was struck by the change in her appearance since their last meeting.

The Politician's kid sister was wan, almost cadaverous, and harried-looking. Her face wore the look, yeah, of a cornered animal. She was drawn and pallid, with dark circles under her eyes.

Toni's shoulder-length dark hair was mussed, looking as though it had been neither washed nor even brushed for several days. And she wore a loose-fitting housecoat, clearly designed to hide her young woman's figure, buttoned high around her throat and trailing almost to the floor.

She greeted them with a weak smile and a breathless monosyllable. Bolan watched her curl into a padded armchair, slim hands clasped tight around her drawn-up knees.

Bolan and Pol sat on the couch opposite, neither of them speaking for a long moment. Bolan used the time to study Toni closely as she sat there, her eyes averted, looking for all the world like a small child peeking through the top of some shapeless tent or sleeping bag.

Where her hands were clenched around her knees, the knuckles were white with tension, fingers tightly interlocked as if to keep those slender hands from trembling.

"I expected you back from the airport sooner," Toni said at last, breaking the awkward silence.

As she spoke, her eyes darted briefly to meet Bolan's, then skittered away again like mice frightened by a sudden noise.

"Yeah, well, we got tied up," the Politician told her.

"Oh?"

Bolan let Toni's brother brief her on their meeting at Holman Field and the violence that followed. Her gaze never returned to him, and he used the opportunity to study her more closely, picking out new lines and shadows that he had never noticed on her face before.

Worry lines, sure. And the shadows of a pain and grief that knows no voice, no expression. She listened to Pol's story.

"What does it mean?" she asked no one in particular.

"Someone is watching Pol," answered Bolan, "or me, or both of us. Beyond that, it's too early to say."

He hesitated briefly before going on.

"I'd like to hear your story before we try putting the pieces together," he finished at last.

At the first mention of her own story, of her troubles, Toni Blancanales paled again, seeming to shrivel inward, withdrawing before Mack Bolan's eyes.

"I don't know how much Rosario has told you," she began at last. "Able Team does a lot of its regular business here in the Twin Cities. You'd be surprised how much of the country's big business is transacted right here."

Rosario broke in, trying to help her out.

"At last estimate, the area was tied with San Francisco for seventh place in the nation as a corporate headquarters site," he said tonelessly.

"You can imagine some of the fierce competition that goes on around here," continued Toni. "Industrial espionage and occasional sabotage, the whole bit. Anyway, we've been working a low-level snooping case, possible pirating of patents, that sort of thing. I had an evening meeting with our client, to pick up some surveillance equipment and collect the final installment of our fee."

"When was this?" Bolan asked softly.

Toni paused, thinking.

"Four days ago now," she answered. "God, it seems like a lifetime."

"Go on, kid," the Politician urged gently.

Toni swallowed hard and said, "Okay. I finished the meeting and went downstairs. The building has one of those underground garages that look like something from *Phantom of the Opera.*

"Anyway, I was stowing our gear in the back seat of my car when this...this man...grabbed me from behind. I never heard him coming.... I never...never...."

She stopped, choking on the words, one hand pressed over her mouth as if she might be ill at any moment. Her dark, hunted eyes stared out through space toward some invisible focal point, watching the nightmare sequence unfold again on a silent mental screen.

"I fought him, believe me, but...he was stronger.... He hit me, Mack, and he forced me into the back seat of the car. He had a knife, and...he said he'd kill me if I didn't...if I didn't...."

Bolan felt a hard fist clenching in his gut, his gorge rising.

"He tore my blouse," she said, "and then... he...made me undress. He...he...oh Jesus."

Sobbing raggedly, the young woman was in fierce pain. But something made her continue, something forced her story to unravel under its own power.

"When he was finished...somehow I knew that he was going to kill me. I *knew* it. He was crazy. I was able...I don't know...somehow I pushed or kicked him out of the car, and I slammed the door shut. I was so afraid of passing out from the pain and the bleeding. He was outside, clawing at the glass like an animal, trying to get in, when...when...."

The words dried up and died. It was as if Toni had lost the thread of thought and was too bone weary to go looking for it again.

After another long moment, Pol composed himself and finished the story for her.

"Our client came down to get his car about that time, Mack, and he scared the stinking son of a bitch away, although he never got a real look at him. Christ almighty, if only he'd been a few minutes earlier!"

"If he had, Toni might not be here," Bolan said gently.

"I've been thinking about that," she murmured, "and you're right. Another minute, either way...." She shuddered and said, "He was willing to kill me. I could feel it."

"Were you able to describe him for the police?" Bolan asked.

The girl nodded jerkily.

"They put together a composite sketch. He

didn't try to hide his face from me. I'm convinced he didn't expect to leave a witness behind."

"So he made a mistake, and the police have something to work with," Bolan said. "What about mug shots?"

Toni tossed her head in a quick negative. "I must have looked at thousands, maybe every bad guy in the Twin Cities. Some were close, but none of them was *him*. Fran says he probably hasn't been arrested before, at least not locally."

"Who's Fran?" Bolan asked.

Toni brightened visibly. "Fran Traynor," she said. "*Officer* Traynor, actually. She heads up a special squad for the St. Paul P.D., specializing in...rape."

"She's been great with Toni," Politician chimed in. "One of those new breed of cops with a special empathy for the victim. I understand she's built her own squad from the ground up, just to handle cases like this."

"God. Cases like this." Toni's voice was hollow as she echoed her brother's words.

Pol moved to kneel beside her, trying to slide a comforting arm around her shoulders, but she twisted away. Rising from her chair, she crossed the room to a bar and poured herself a stiff drink from the lone bottle that was standing there.

Pol looked after her with hurting eyes, then turned again to Bolan.

"The police are the problem, Mack," he said as he sat down again. "I mean, for the first day or so, everyone was all gung ho to find this animal and take him off the streets. Officer Traynor and her team seemed to be right on top of the case."

Bolan was curious. "So what happened?"

Blancanales shrugged helplessly.

"Damned if I know. As soon as Toni gave her description to the police artist, you could feel the ice forming. All of a sudden the faces started changing, and Traynor was out. There's this big bull...."

"Detective Foss, or something," Toni interjected from the bar. "I don't remember."

"Right," Pol confirmed, nodding. "He comes on to Toni like she can't trust her own eyes and her description's not worth a damn. I swear to God, he made it sound like she...like she *asked* for it, Mack."

Pol was furious now, eyes glazing and fists clenched as he finished.

"I finally told him to stay the hell away from her," he grated. "And we haven't heard a word from St. Paul's finest since then."

"I can't put my finger on anything specific," Toni added, "but I believe the police are hiding something."

Pol was shaking his head in dazed wonder, like a punchy fighter.

"I can't fathom any of this," he said, bewildered. "Why? What reason could they possibly have for protecting an animal like that?"

Bolan raised a cautious eyebrow.

"We don't know that anyone *is* protecting him, Pol. Not yet. I trust Toni's instincts, but we need a lot more to accuse the police of whitewashing rape and attempted murder. If we can prove a cover-up, we'll have the motive. If we can't. . . ."

He left the statement hanging, unfinished.

It was Toni's turn.

"Then you'll have one paranoid woman, right?" she said, growing angry now. "Well, I'm not paranoid, dammit. I'm not!"

Bolan raised both hands in a soothing, pacifying gesture.

"Okay," he agreed, "so we start digging. And along the way, maybe we'll find out why those guns were waiting for us at the airport."

"Where do we start?" Pol asked.

"You stay here with Toni," Bolan told him. "She's been through enough already, and if someone is calling out the guns, we don't want her alone."

Blancanales nodded quickly. "Right, right. What about you?"

"I'd like to see how Officer Traynor feels about being frozen out of the case. Do you know how I can contact her? Preferably off the job."

"Yes, just a minute," Toni told him.

She produced a small white business card. It bore Fran Traynor's name and precinct telephone number, with a home number penciled in below.

"She told me to call her anytime," Toni said softly, "but since everything's changed. . . I didn't want to make things any worse."

Bolan rose to leave, pocketing the card and glancing at his wristwatch.

"It looks like I'll have to wake her up," he said,

then turned to Pol. "You have a way to keep in touch?"

Blancanales grinned, nodding. "I've got just the thing," he said, striding quickly off into the second bedroom.

With her brother gone, Toni seemed to shrink another few inches into herself. Mack Bolan moved closer to her.

"Try to get some rest," he said. "And leave everything else to me."

He reached out to rest one hand on her frail shoulder, but she jerked away, her mouth was suddenly tight, eyes wary, darting from side to side as if in search of an escape exit.

As Bolan regarded her closely for a moment, the trapped expression softened, and there was the glint of tears behind long eyelashes.

"I'm sorry, Mack," she said bitterly, "I. . . I just can't."

Pol Blancanales chose that moment to return. Sensing the tension in the room, he tried to defuse it, holding out one of a pair of compact radios he carried.

"A little something I cooked up in my spare time," he said, grinning at Bolan. "Boosted the range and whatnot. Inside of thirty miles you should read five-by-five."

Bolan pocketed the tiny transceiver and shook hands with his friend, saying hushed goodbyes before he let himself out.

He took the stairs two at a time on his way to the Politician's rented car.

There was no limit, it seemed, to the number of victims. Hell, it was always open season on the weak, the meek, and the good, whether predators were stalking the streets and alleys or the steaming jungles of the world.

And no limit on the human capacity for suffering.

Someone close to Mack Bolan was suffering now, and that someone had damn sure suffered enough.

Someone else, though, had not yet begun to suffer for the pain he had inflicted on others.

There was inequity there, right enough, and the Executioner meant to do everything in his power to balance the scales a bit. Maybe, just maybe, he would have the luck and the odds that he needed on his side to upset those bloody scales completely.

At least for a little while.

No war, it seems, ever is won. It only pauses to rest before breaking out again, somewhere else, under some other flag or justification. Today the battlefield was St. Paul. Tomorrow. . . ?

Bolan put the grim thoughts from his mind and concentrated on his unscheduled meeting with a lady cop.

5

Bolan checked Fran Traynor's name and number against a St. Paul telephone directory and came up lucky. Unlike many police officers, who opted for unlisted phone numbers, the lady cop was listed on what turned out to be a medium-prosperous residential street lined with tract houses and scattered shade trees. At that hour of the morning, all the houses were sleeping, cloaked in darkness.

On his first drive-by, Bolan noted that the house's separate garage was set well back and away from the road. There were two cars in the driveway. A small foreign compact was parked nose-on toward the big garage door, and a long black Cadillac had it blocked, filling the drive behind it.

So the lady had company, or else she liked to drive in style.

Bolan couldn't see an honest cop laying out the necessary cash for the big Detroit black, so it remained to be seen only if Fran Traynor's company was welcome or unexpected.

And the Executioner suddenly had a strong negative feeling about that Caddy in the driveway.

He had seen too many like it before, sure, during his home-front war against the Mafia octopus, to avoid a warning tightness in his gut at the sight of the big steel shark waiting silently, as if for prey.

And yet he could not afford to jump to any conclusions, either. It was just that he could never be too careful if he wanted to keep on breathing and walking around with all his working parts in operating condition. Not after the greeting he and Pol had received a few hours earlier.

Bolan drove on by the apparently sleeping house and parked his rental car two houses down. Within seconds he had checked the load on the 9mm Beretta Brigadier beneath his left arm, and he was E.V.A., moving through the darkness like a wraith as he backtracked toward the home of the lady cop.

He entered her yard, which was wrapped in deepest shadow, and it didn't take thirty seconds to confirm his worst suspicions.

A cigarette was bobbing and glowing in the driver's seat of the black Cadillac. It did not take any combat genius to decide that a friend or lover spending the night with a lady would not leave his chauffeur waiting at the wheel.

The car was a crew wagon. If not Mafia, then some deadly affiliate. And it looked as if the driver was expecting his crew back at the car at any moment.

Mack Bolan decided not to keep the guy waiting any longer.

Sliding the Beretta Belle from its side leather sheath, Bolan made a stealthy approach to within arm's length of the driver's window. Even with the iron-clad certainty of experience and intuition burning in his mind, he refused to snipe the guy from a distance without making positive, final verification of his allegiance and identity.

The Executioner would have no innocent blood on his soul.

And from five feet away, he knew that his intuition still functioned, his combat instincts were still finely honed and working smoothly.

The guy *was* syndicate. There was no mistaking the bulge of holstered hardware beneath the left arm. And even in the darkness, there was no mistaking the type, either. The thirty-dollar haircut and the expensive suit that somehow never matched the swarthy face of a street-wise, slumborn punk.

And yeah, Bolan was certain. But he had to be certain in his soul, where it counted, as well as in his mind and in his gut. There would have to be one last, indisputable test.

Bolan made the split-second decision, recognizing all possible consequences in the space of a heartbeat. If his instincts were wrong, and the guy was a lawman or an armed civilian bodyguard of some sort, he would have to withdraw as best he could and contact Fran Traynor another time. If he was right. . . .

Bolan moved. He stepped out of the shrubbery, deliberately exposing himself and holding the

Beretta out of sight along his thigh. The driver saw him at once, and his boredom vanished in a fast double-take. His reaction was swift, practiced, and it sealed his fate. The sawed-off shotgun that came nosing up over the dash told Bolan all he needed to know.

No cop or trained security man would react in such a fashion, without warning, and none would have armed himself with such a weapon. The guy was dirty, all right. And he was dead.

Bolan extended the Beretta to arm's length, the squat muzzle of its special silencer a foot from the wheelman's face, and he stroked the trigger lightly. The shotgun muzzle continued to rise and level out. The Belle coughed out a single breathless *phut*. The driver slumped sideways in his seat, the cigarette a fading ember now on the bloodspattered floorboards of the Caddy.

Bolan moved on, rounding the rear of Fran Traynor's house and finding the back door unlocked. From that angle, he could also see that lights were burning inside, although they had been invisible from the street.

The Executioner entered the house silently, moving through a cluttered utility area and down a hallway, following the source of illumination. The silenced Beretta nosed its cautious way ahead of him, ready for trouble.

At last he stood beside a partially open bathroom door, poised and listening, his every combat sense alert. From beyond that threshold came the sound of water and the low mutter of voices, as if someone within was washing clothes by hand and talking to himself.

Bolan risked a glance around the doorjamb, taking in the whole scene immediately.

Two hardmen, both in shirtsleeves, knelt beside the porcelain bathtub. Their jackets had been laid carefully aside, their sleeves rolled up above the elbows to avoid becoming drenched as the men went about their task.

They were drowning a naked woman in the tub.

Almost reluctantly, it seemed to Bolan, they would dunk the blonde head under water and hold it there, strong hands subduing what were minimal struggles at best. He guessed that the woman had been drugged or otherwise rendered semiconscious as a prelude to her watery execution.

And they kept dragging her up again from beneath the water's surface, shaking her as if they sought to keep her at least partially sentient and aware throughout the ordeal. Bolan caught a quick glimpse of a flushed face half-hidden by a screen of sodden hair, and the roundness of one breast before the lady was submerged again.

And close up now, he could understand the words spoken by the two rental ghouls.

"I still say it's a shame all of this has to go to waste," the one on the left was saying with a leer.

"Forget it, stud," the guy's partner snapped. "This is supposed to look like an accident, not an orgy."

"A goddamned shame," the first guy grunted, bending to his task with renewed vigor.

Mack Bolan had seen and heard enough. He stepped through the doorway, the Belle up at full extension and steadied in a two-handed grip for optimum accuracy in rapid fire. He nudged the bathroom door wide open with one foot, and the hinges gave out a tiny squeak of response.

One of the gunmen was half turned toward him, growling, "Dammit, Joey, I told you to stay—" The kneeling man saw not Joey, but the dark, grim specter of Death poised in the doorway, ready to collect its dues.

The guy's mouth dropped open, emitting a strangled sound somewhere between a curse and a prayer.

Neither helped.

The Beretta Belle chugged once, the 9mm bone-crusher impacting between startled eyes and bouncing the man off the side of the tub, draping him over the toilet bowl. The back of his skull gleamed sticky red in the artificial lighting.

Hit man number two was at last aware, in the slow motion of crisis, of something terribly wrong in the bathroom. He twisted in his crouch, one wet hand clawing at the .38 snubby on his right hip.

He never made it.

Bolan shot him through the throat. Then a second parabellum slug ripped through his temple to core his brain and explode on the other side in a shower of bone and tissue.

Moving swiftly, Bolan sheathed the hot Brigadier and moved to the side of the tub. Reaching down, he snared the naked lady still submerged there, and hauled her, coughing, out of a watery grave.

She was very naked, yeah. And there was a single purple bruise on her right temple.

The hit man's words came back to him, loud and clear.

It's supposed to look like an accident.

So the bruise was meant to give a touch of authenticity to an ordinary bathtub fall and accidental drowning. Once the place was checked for prints and found squeaky clean, not even Fran Traynor's friends on the P.D. would have cause to look any further for an alternate solution.

It was a slick plan, if not exactly original. Slick and professional. But that was the least of the problems.

Problem number one was clinging to Bolan's arm for dear life, sucking wind like a drowned rat and shivering in the half-conscious knowledge that she had somehow been saved.

Bolan led the lady on shaky legs out of the bloody shambles of her bathroom and into an adjoining bedroom, where he flicked on the lights and deposited her in an upright position on the bed. He had snared some towels on the way, and now he began briskly drying her off from head to toe. As he worked, he noted the return of healthy color to her pale flesh.

Her first feeble protest was swallowed in another fit of coughing that brought up more water from her lungs, but within moments she was strong enough to wrench the towel away from him and hold it in front of herself as a shield for her nudity.

Bolan left her there, breathing heavily, one of her hands pressed to her head and the other holding the bath towel against her breasts.

He moved quickly, finding the kitchen and scanning the household items beneath the sink. He found a fat roll of paper towels, some rags, and a half-empty box of plastic trash can liners, then took all the items back to the bathroom slaughterhouse with him.

After sliding an extra-strength trash bag over the mangled upper quarters of each lifeless man, Bolan set about swabbing the walls and tub area with the paper towels, careful to expunge all vestiges of blood and tissue.

He did not intend to leave any trace of the two hired killers behind.

When he was finished, he gave the whole room a quick visual inspection, then shoved the bloody towels inside one of the laden trash bags. As a last step, he rifled the pockets of the dead men, coming up with drivers' licenses that identified them as Philip Ciccio and Joseph Lupo, respectively.

Bolan pocketed the ID cards and moved back to the bedroom doorway. Inside, Fran Traynor was standing beside the bed, a large bath towel draped across her, toga-fashion, hiding her shapely form from collarbone to upper thighs. Still a bit unsteady, she stood with one slim hand braced against the edge of a bedside nightstand.

And the other hand was clenched tightly around a snub-nosed .38 special.

Aimed right at Mack Bolan.

"You don't need that," he said. "I'm not the enemy."

"So you say." Her voice was firm, no longer waterlogged.

Bolan shrugged impassively. "If I wanted you dead, I could have done it in there." He jerked a thumb over his shoulder toward the bathroom beyond. "Or I could have let Mutt and Jeff finish what they started."

There was a trace of uncertainty in the lady cop's eyes now, and the stubby muzzle of her weapon slipped a notch lower, freezing somewhere on a level with the Executioner's groin.

"So. . . who *are* you?" she asked at last. "*What* are you?"

Bolan moved a cautious step forward before the .38 snapped up again to freeze him in his tracks.

"An ally, Fran. Perhaps a friend."

For the first time that night, the lady cop looked not frightened or exhausted, but honestly surprised.

"I didn't drop in here tonight by accident," Bolan assured her. "I came looking for you."

The gun was slipping lower again, and Bolan sidled another step closer, farther into the room.

"So did those two in there," Fran Traynor retorted. "Are they both. . . dead?"

Bolan nodded. "We have to start thinking about who sent them after you, and why."

"We?"

She clearly was having a hard time accepting this dark stranger as a friend, even though he had just saved her life.

"I'm an ally," Bolan repeated patiently. "For the moment, your enemies are mine."

"Who are you?" she asked again. She was sounding increasingly desperate.

"We can talk about that after I finish cleaning up and get you safely out of here," he said.

The .38's hammer snapped back into full cock under her thumb.

"I'm not going anywhere, and neither are they," she said sharply. Her gun flicked away in a swift gesture toward the bathroom and its lifeless tenants.

Bolan forced a casual shrug. "Suit yourself. If you'd rather wait here for the backup team. . . ."

Fran Traynor tossed her head defiantly, flinging wet strands of hair back from her face.

"I can take care of myself, Mr. . . . whatever. And I can have a police squad here within minutes."

Bolan nodded toward the bathroom. "Those guys were puppets, Fran. Think about it. I wouldn't make any calls until I found out who's been pulling the strings."

That shocked her, and the .38's muzzle did a rapid slide in the direction of Bolan's ankles. He knew that he could take it from her easily, but he let her keep it.

"What do you suggest?" she asked after a long pause.

"First, you get dressed. Meanwhile, I take out the trash, and then together we find you a safe place to stay. After that, we must talk."

Bolan left her to get dressed, and returned to the bathroom and the two corpses laid out head-first in the garbage bags. He carried them out to the waiting Caddy one at a time, slung over his shoulder in the traditional fireman's carry. Outside, the ignition yielded up a key, and he dumped each man in turn into the trunk. Joey the driver joined them in that ignominious pile.

Trusting that Fran was confused and frightened enough to heed his advice and stay off the telephone, Bolan spared more precious numbers to fire up the Cadillac's engine and pilot the big crew wagon down the block to the next intersection. He left it sitting beside the trash dumpsters of an all-night quick-stop market, and locked the keys inside.

Walking back, he retrieved his rental car and parked it in the Caddy's former place in Fran Traynor's driveway. A quick glance down the street showed him lights newly turned on in two of the houses, but there was no other sign of activity.

They wouldn't have much time to waste, even so. He meant to be out of there with the lady cop before being observed by any of the early-rising neighbors, or police cruisers.

When he reentered the house, Bolan found Fran Traynor dressed and ready to go. She was waiting for him in the bedroom, a purse and overnight bag on the bed beside her. The snubby .38 was nowhere in evidence.

"I didn't know when I'd be coming back, so. . . ." She gestured toward the bags, leaving the sentence unfinished.

"Good idea," Bolan agreed. "And I hope it won't be for long."

"Let's go," she said, sounding suddenly disinterested, preoccupied. "It doesn't feel homey here right now."

6

Bolan and Fran Traynor drove in mutual silence to a comfortable motel set back several blocks from the tangle of downtown St. Paul. Bolan registered with a sleepy, disinterested desk clerk, signing the registry for Mr. and Mrs. Frank La Mancha. It was a name he would be using to significant effect in the events to come. Bolan then parked his rented sedan in front of a room at the far end of the motel's east wing.

He locked the door behind them and turned to find the lady cop standing beside the double bed, facing him, digging something out of her purse.

He sighed. "I thought we'd gotten beyond the gun."

Her cheeks colored as she produced a leather billfold and snapped it open, flashing her gold detective's shield into view.

"I want you to know who you're dealing with," she said.

"I know who you are, Fran. I told you."

She looked attractive as she very promptly became flustered.

"Well...damn!" was the best she could manage. She sat down on the edge of the bed.

Bolan spoke after a long pause. He was looking at her intently. "There are some questions I have to ask you."

"Not so fast, handsome." She raised a cautioning hand. "I've got about a zillion questions of my own, starting with who you are, and I am not in the best of health and humor, in case you hadn't noticed. . . ."

Bolan appreciated her spirit as much as her good looks. She was plucky enough to endure a deadly and humiliating ordeal, and then play cop. She was strong inside.

"The name I used to register will do for now," he told her. "Let's just say that our paths crossed at an opportune moment."

"Opportune for *me*," she said. "Why for you?"

Bolan shrugged, dropping into a chair beside the bed.

"If you're dead, you can't answer those questions," he said simply.

"I may not answer anyway."

"You haven't heard them yet."

"Okay."

Bolan paused briefly.

"I need some information on one of your cases," he began.

Her eyes narrowed slightly.

"Which case?" she asked stiffly.

"The Blancanales rape."

It was as if he had slapped her across the face. She tried to regain her composure at once, but the effect of his words was obvious.

"What's your interest?" she asked finally. She was going to stall.

"Let's say I'm interested in justice."

"You must know I can't divulge information in a rape case," she said. Her voice had become confidential, even though they were clearly alone. "You're wasting your time."

"I don't want the lurid stuff," he said. "I'm not interested in it. My interest lies in what's being done to close the case."

It took her some moments to consider what he had just said. She averted her eyes as she answered.

"A rape can be one of the hardest cases to break, especially where the perpetrator is a stranger to the victim."

"Or when someone upstairs is running interference?"

He had timed that bomb deliberately. He watched her face closely. He saw what he was looking for—angry fire in her eyes... and something more, deep down, when her head snapped up to meet his cool gaze directly.

"What? Now, look, I don't think we should continue—"

"Why were you dumped from the rape squad, Fran?" He asked it softly. "Why now, instead of last month or next year?"

She was stunned.

"Listen, Mr. Whoever, I wasn't...."

She paused in mid-sentence. Then her shoulders seemed to sag, as if she was tired from carrying the weight of the world.

"So, okay," she said. "I was dumped."

"Why?"

She shook her head firmly, sending her barely dry blonde curls into shimmering motion around her face.

"No. You're asking me to reveal department business for a civilian who won't even give me his name."

Bolan fished a nondescript Justice Department ID card out of a breast pocket and skimmed it across to her. It carried the La Mancha alias and was one of the many traveling papers prepared for him by the machinery housed at Stony Man Farm. The card would confirm an identity and official position for him. It was as crucial a device, in many ways, as any weapon in his armory of hardware.

"I'm not a curiosity seeker," he said firmly.

Fran examined the card, then looked at him quizzically.

"What's the federal interest in Toni Blancanales?" she asked.

"None. We were talking about police suppression of evidence."

The worried look returned.

"Well..." the lady cop began, "*I* never said that. Don't put words in my mouth, okay?"

"Why were you transferred, Fran?"

"I'm not sure. They called it a promotion, of course, increased departmental status and so on. Goodbye rape unit. I was put into public relations."

Bolan cocked an eyebrow. "You didn't request the move?"

She shook her head, a firm negative.

"They told me about their great need for women in the upper echelons, et cetera, all for the good of the department, you know? And look at the trouble it's got me into already," she added, holding herself to avoid involuntary shivers.

"Who's they?"

"What? Oh, Jack Fawcett, mainly. That's Lieutenant Fawcett, homicide division."

"Does he normally hand out promotions and transfers?"

"The promotion came from upstairs."

"How high?" Bolan asked.

"Sorry. No idea."

"What were you working on when the transfer came down?"

Fran Traynor hesitated. She was obviously reluctant to answer further questions. But looking into his eyes, she found something there that encouraged her to open up.

"I have this theory about. . . well, in the past thirty months or so, there have been five identical rape-murders here in St. Paul."

It was Bolan's turn to show surprise.

"Identical?"

She nodded animatedly.

"Virtually," she confirmed. "Of course, I'm the only one who seems to think so. But I swear, the M.O.'s are carbon copy. All five victims were found nude, multiple assaults, their throats slashed, and. . . well, other mutilations."

"And Homicide sees no similarity?"

"Oh, Lieutenant Fawcett will admit certain common elements," she answered, "but he insists that the time factor rules out a single perpetrator."

"How's that?"

"Well, the first killing came eleven months before the next two, and then eighteen months went by before the final pair. Once they start killing, your headcases normally go at it nonstop until they burn out or take the fall. One-third of all murderers end up as suicides, as a matter of fact—"

"But you have a theory." He was still standing before her as she sat, still exhausted from her ordeal, on the motel bed.

"I believe the intervals between crimes occur when the killer is interrupted, probably by arrest on other charges, or by commitment to an institution," she explained. "Now, the intervals seem too short and irregular for normal sentencing and parole, so—"

"An escapee," Bolan finished for her. The old tightness was back in his gut.

"Exactly," she said, almost shouting it out. "If I can find a man who was locked up during the relevant periods but escaped in time to commit each of the murders . . . I've got him!"

"What's your progress?" the Executioner asked.

She looked downcast again, losing some of the exhilaration.

"Negative on all local jail records," she said. "I was just starting a canvass of mental institutions when I got kicked upstairs. But from the rapist's M.O.—as far as he got, that is—I believe it is the same man who got Toni Blancanales, and I believe that Toni is the only living eyewitness."

"Who is in charge of the Blancanales investigation now?" he asked.

"Well...Lieutenant Fawcett has indirect authority, in conjunction with someone from the rape unit."

"How does Homicide inherit a rape case?"

She smiled wryly. "R.H.I.P., mister. Rank hath its privileges."

"So what happens to your pet theory, Fran?"

"I still have my friends on the unit," she said. "A transfer doesn't change that. Between us, we'll finish the canvass of sanitariums sooner or later."

"Make it sooner," Bolan advised sternly.

The lady cop bristled visibly at that.

"You don't rank me, mister. I don't know why I'm spilling my guts to you anyway, when I don't even know your interest in all this."

"I told you, I'm interested in justice," Bolan said. "And if your theory proves out, there's more to all this than a sex freak on the prowl. I'll need a copy of that suspect sketch, and any pertinent data from your canvass."

The lady cop stiffened.

"You ask a lot, La Mancha. You won't get me to hurt the department."

"I haven't asked you to. But *if* there is a cover-up, then those responsible are spoiling every decent thing a lawman stands for. You owe them nothing."

There was another long pause. "I'll have to think this over," she said.

Bolan nodded.

"You know the numbers," he said softly. "Our man missed with Toni, so he's still hungry. How long have we got?"

"Give me time to think, dammit!" she snapped. There was more worry than anger in her voice.

Bolan wrote a telephone number, Pol's answering service, on a card and then rose to leave.

"You can reach me through this number when you make up your mind. And you might watch your step today."

"Bet on it," she told him, smiling again. "And thanks...for happening by. You know, I should report what happened."

"I recommend you don't for now," said Bolan. "See if anybody acts surprised. I'll direct Lieutenant Fawcett to your visitors when I see him."

And with that he left her, passing back into the early-morning darkness that was already tinged with faint traces of gray on the eastern horizon. He had spent more time with the lady cop than he had planned—but he felt that the time had been well spent.

Even so, he had damned little to work with and, possibly, even less time to seek his handle on the situation. If Fran Traynor's theory proved out... and if there was a smoke screen being laid downtown....

Too damned many *if*'s, yeah.

Still, he could project areas of caution and concern, even with the small amount of solid data available.

Item: Someone had definitely called out the guns, and unless they played industrial espionage for keeps in the Twin Cities, that meant someone was vitally interested in Toni's case.

Item: By logical extension, and if Fran was right about Toni being the only living witness to a mass killer's identity, then the shadowy someone just might want Blancanales's sister taken out of the picture permanently.

And finally, Item: By all indications, the human savage that Bolan had come to St. Paul to eliminate was still out there, hungry and waiting for his next chance to strike. And if the lady cop was correct in her surmising, he was not only a rapist, but a five-time murderer as well.

7

Lieutenant Jack Fawcett was tired and exasperated, and he didn't care who knew it.

He didn't like being roused from sleep in the predawn hours to drive across town and stand above the remains of two leaking stiffs, even though the assignment was nothing new or extraordinary for a lieutenant in homicide division. It was still a drag, even after fourteen years on the job. It would always be a drag.

He watched the uniformed officers moving listlessly as they herded the little clutch of sleepy residents back from the crime scene and onto the sidewalk. All around the little cul-de-sac, people in bathrobes and slippers were sprinkled across lawns and sidewalks, gawking morbidly at the silent residue of violent death.

Behind Fawcett, to the east, the sky was showing the faintest line of pink along the horizon. On the little residential street it was still dark, however, the scene lit eerily by the flashing lights of black and white police units and the city tow truck he had ordered up.

If Jack Fawcett couldn't sleep, hell, nobody would sleep.

The tow truck had just finished winching the long sedan over and onto its tires again from its previous inverted position. The medical examiner's two orderlies were removing a limp body from the driver's seat, laying it out on the street for preliminary examination. To Fawcett's right, in the middle of the street, a second prone figure lay shrouded in linen.

A young junior-grade detective approached Fawcett. His youthful face was already hardened around the eyes and mouth from exposure to violent death. He carried a large manila envelope, the contents jingling, and popped it open to show Fawcett a glittering pile of shell casings inside.

"Nine millimeter," the young detective said. "We picked up a couple dozen back there." He jerked his thumb over one shoulder to indicate the middle of the cul-de-sac.

Fawcett grunted in reply, unwilling to waste words on the obvious.

The young detective wouldn't be put off. He was anxious to display his knowledge and professionalism for the ranking officer on the scene.

"Probably an Uzi," he began, "or a Smith and Wesson M-79. Of course, it could have been—"

"What about the D.O.A.'s?" Fawcett interrupted gruffly. "Were they packing?"

The young cop faltered, breaking his verbal stride, finally nodding.

"Uh, that's affirmative," he said. "We found a silenced .380 back where the vehicle started its roll, and the driver's wearing a .45. The .380's been fired recently."

Fawcett allowed himself a small, sardonic grin.

"Turkey shoot," he said softly to himself.

"How's that?"

Fawcett scowled, scanning the crime scene with narrowed eyes and a pointing index finger.

"See for yourself," he said. "These cocks came barreling in here, hell for leather and ready to rip. Only they weren't ready enough."

"A mob hit?" the younger man asked, sounding excited.

Fawcett shrugged wearily. "What else?"

It was the young cop's turn to frown.

"Well. . . maybe radicals . . . or . . . ."

Fawcett snorted. "When was the last time you saw radicals riding around after midnight in fancy suits? Jesus."

The young man's face reddened; he half turned away from the lieutenant, trying to hide his embarrassment from his superior officer. Fawcett sensed that he was on the verge of making an enemy and pulled back, his tone softening.

"Listen," he said more gently, "why don't you finish inspecting the scene and get started on your report. You know how to handle it?"

The young detective brightened immediately as he realized he was being placed in temporary charge of the investigation.

"Yes, sir," he snapped, almost standing at attention. "I'll get right on it."

He hurried off, barking orders at a pair of uniformed patrolmen and bustling around personally to examine the ruined hulk of an automobile.

Fawcett ambled over to where the middle-aged

coroner's assistant, an old acquaintance and sometime friend, was crouched beside the dead man from the car. As he approached, the M.E. glanced up and shot him a sarcastic grin of welcome.

"Well, now," he said, "I thought you were working days."

Fawcett treated the guy to one of his best scowls.

"I'm working when they call me. Somebody thinks this one's special, I guess."

The medical examiner cocked an eyebrow.

"Somebody could be right. I haven't seen one like this in...oh, two, three years."

"Do I need to ask the cause of death?" Fawcett inquired listlessly.

The M.E. straightened up, knee joints popping like small-arms fire.

"Take your pick," he said amiably. "Multiple bullet wounds to head and chest, obvious internal injuries from the crash. They had a rough night, Jack."

"You read this as an organization thing?" Fawcett asked, lowering his voice slightly.

The medical examiner nodded. "Gotta be. Who else plays these kinds of games?"

"Nobody," Fawcett answered wearily. "I'll need a copy of that report."

The examiner smiled and lit a cigarette, blowing the smoke in Fawcett's direction.

"Right now, or just immediately?"

"Everybody's a comedian," the homicide lieutenant growled, turning away and walking back to his unmarked cruiser.

He had reached the vehicle and had one hand on the door when a big man dressed with expensive good taste materialized beside him, as if out of thin air. Fawcett blinked twice, glancing rapidly around the scene and wondering where in hell the guy had come from.

"Jack Fawcett?" the big guy asked, smiling thinly.

The lieutenant's eyes narrowed with instinctive suspicion.

"Who's asking?"

The big guy flashed an official-looking card, then pocketed it again before Fawcett could focus on it.

"La Mancha, Justice Department," he said, smile fading. "We need to talk."

Fawcett exhaled heavily. "It figures."

The big guy raised a curious eyebrow. "How's that?"

"Sure, whenever the wise guys start to burn each other, the federales are never far behind."

The man called La Mancha nodded toward the cluster of officers and rubberneckers around the battered crew wagon.

"You're calling this a syndicate hit?" he asked.

"Hell, yes," Fawcett snapped. "It's got all the signs."

The big guy was circling Fawcett's cruiser, already climbing in on the passenger side as he said, "Let's take a ride. I'm parked around the corner."

Cursing softly, angered by the fed's take-charge attitude, Lieutenant Fawcett slid behind the wheel, fired the cruiser's engine, and put the unmarked car in motion.

"The Twin Cities are supposed to be quiet, Jack," La Mancha said when they were rolling.

Fawcett shrugged, further annoyed by the first name familiarity.

"Sure, sure, but hell, who can figure these animals? Probably they got mixed up in some damned vendetta or something."

"Maybe."

The big fed's tone was clearly skeptical.

Fawcett bristled, shooting a sidelong glance toward his uninvited passenger.

"You don't think so?"

La Mancha avoided the question, changing the subject.

"How's business in homicide, Jack?"

Taken by surprise, Fawcett blinked rapidly, putting his thoughts in working order.

"Huh? Aw, nothing special. Why?"

"I understand you've got yourself a headcase who doesn't like the ladies."

Just like that, cool as you please. Fawcett stiffened in the driver's seat, hoping at once that it didn't show. He felt his guts going into a slow barrel roll.

"First I've heard of it," he answered after a moment, fighting to keep the tightness and hostility out of his voice.

"Really?"

The goddamned guy next to him was all cool, calm, and collected, sitting there calling Jack Fawcett a liar without really saying so. The lieutenant began to see red and fought the feeling down. He swung the cruiser in to curbside and stood on the brake, forcing an even tone into his voice as he turned toward La Mancha.

"What the hell is this all about?" he demanded. "What does the organized crime unit want with a headcase?"

"Who said I work the org crime unit?"

The damned guy was smiling at him!

Fawcett's insides completed their roll. He felt dizzy.

"Well . . . I just assumed. . . ."

The federal man's smile broadened, without gaining any warmth.

"You know what they say about assumptions, Jack."

"Well, what do you want?"

"I'm with SOG," La Mancha said simply. "Sensitive Operations Group."

Fawcett was nonplussed.

"I, uh, guess I'm not familiar with that unit," he said.

"It's need-to-know, Jack. You don't."

Fawcett felt as if he had been slapped.

"So, okay," he said, forcing a casual tone he didn't feel, "why are we having this conversation?"

"I was asking you about your problem. The headcase."

"And I'm telling you that there isn't any god-damned headache. I don't know where you get your information—"

"That's right," the big guy cut him off, still smiling. "You don't."

Jack Fawcett felt like a tire with the air slowly leaking out of it.

"Listen, La Mancha, somebody's been feeding you a line. There's no way I wouldn't know about something like that."

"That's what I thought," La Mancha said, nodding.

Fawcett's hands fidgeted on the steering wheel like nervous spiders.

"Okay," he said. "So you asked, and I told you. That's it, right?"

"We'll see."

"Well, what the hell—"

"About those D.O.A.'s, you may need to rethink the syndicate connection."

Fawcett was on firmer ground now, and he felt some of his old self-confidence returning.

"Says who?"

"Call it intuition," the fed replied. "While you're at it, you might want to pick up the other three."

He was already out of the car and leaning in through the passenger's window, big forearms neatly crossed on the frame.

Fawcett was flustered now, hopelessly confused.

"Other three what?" he asked.

"Bodies, Jack," La Mancha said patiently.

And the man called La Mancha proceeded to tell the dumbfounded Jack Fawcett exactly where and how to find a Caddy with three cold ones in the trunk. Fawcett had just enough presence of mind to memorize the details for future use.

"You have to get on the right side of this thing, Lieutenant," La Mancha was saying from the window. "We don't want to see a career man get caught with his pants down."

Jack Fawcett felt numb.

"I don't know what you're talking about, mister."

The federale's smile was back in place.

"Okay. I'll be in touch in case you change your mind."

And Fawcett was still trying to think up a snappy retort to that when he noticed that the big guy was gone. He craned his neck, catching a brief glimpse of the man's retreating back in the rearview mirror before he disappeared entirely. After another long moment, Fawcett came to himself and put the cruiser in casual, aimless motion.

I understand you've got yourself a headcase.

Jack Fawcett cursed, softly and fluently. It would be the homicide lieutenant's job to find out how much this guy knew and where he was getting his information.

And along the way, he might have to check up and see just who Mr. No-Name La Mancha really was. That Justice Department ID looked okay at first glance, and yet. . . .

Another thought came to Jack Fawcett, banishing all others in an instant.

He would have to get in touch with the commissioner, no doubt about that. And no delaying it, either.

He checked his watch, wincing at what it told him.

The commissioner wouldn't like being roused from a sound sleep this early in the morning. When you reached his station in life, you were accustomed to something like bankers' hours.

Fawcett grinned mirthlessly to himself. *If I don't sleep, nobody sleeps,* he thought.

But he didn't feel the bravado, not down inside where his guts were still quaking and shifting.

And he wasn't looking forward to his next encounter of the morning. Not one damned bit.

8

Mack Bolan, alias John Phoenix and lately Frank La Mancha of Washington, came away from his meeting with Jack Fawcett convinced that the homicide lieutenant was hiding a great deal.

But what?

Bolan had clearly touched a raw nerve with his "headcase" remarks. And while it was a long way from proving the veteran cop's involvement in a murder cover-up, Fawcett's reaction to that probe definitely warranted a deeper look.

The big guy touched base with Pol Blancanales via the compact radio transceiver. He raised his old friend on the second try.

"Able One," Pol's tinny voice responded. "I read you, Stony Man, over."

"What's the condition of our patient?" Bolan asked.

"Anything but," came the answer. "She's climbing the walls here."

"Keep the lid on, Able. I'm rattling cages right now."

"Uh, you may be hitting paydirt, Stony Man," his old friend said. "We just heard from the lady law, and she wants a parley with La Mancha, soonest."

"Name the place," Bolan said.

Blancanales gave him the address of a twenty-four-hour restaurant just off Kellogg Boulevard. He said Fran Traynor had left a number and was waiting to roll when she received Bolan's call-back.

The Executioner checked his wristwatch.

"Have her there in fifteen, Able."

"Roger that," Pol acknowledged. "Fifteen it is."

"Any feelings on the lady?"

After a pause, the metallic voice came back.

"Nothing firm. She sounded shaky, though. Right down to the ground."

"Okay. How do you stand with the people at Motor Vehicles?"

"I've got an in," Blancanales said. "Got some numbers for me?"

"Affirmative."

Bolan rattled off the license numbers of the chase car they had wrecked earlier that morning, and the Cadillac crew wagon he had found at Fran's residence.

"I need that soonest," he added.

"I'm on it now. Able out."

Bolan laid the little radio aside and put his rented car into a tight U-turn at the next intersection.

He wondered what had happened since their brief encounter, to shake up Fran Traynor any more than the appearance of three gunmen bent on murder in the small hours of the morning. Finally, unable to divine the answer, he quit trying.

If the lady came through with the information he needed, it might just be Bolan's turn to do some shaking in the Twin Cities. And he was ready to shake somebody at that moment, shake them hard.

Right down to the ground.

Assistant Police Commissioner Roger Smalley was awake earlier than usual, and he was disgruntled by the call from Detective Lieutenant Jack Fawcett.

Fawcett had sounded nervous on the phone, hardly making sense, in fact, so Smalley had reluctantly told him to come on over and relate his problem in person. Now, with his wife sleeping upstairs, Smalley sat in his rather luxurious study, smoking his first cigar of the new day.

Commissioner Smalley was not unfamiliar with wake-up calls, both from his superiors and, less often, from his subordinates. But now, at age fifty-two, one step removed from the pinnacle of power in St. Paul's police establishment, the superiors were fewer in number, and subordinates were well advised to hold their calls until office hours.

It would have to be something special, really extraordinary, for Jack Fawcett to call and wake him at sunrise, demanding a face-to-face meeting. And because it would be something special, something extraordinary, Roger Smalley was not only feeling disgruntled. He was feeling nervous.

The assistant commissioner would humor Jack Fawcett—to a point. But he hoped for the lieutenant's sake that Fawcett wasn't letting the strain of his job get the better of him.

Yeah, it had damned well better be something extraordinary.

Smalley heard the soft knock on the side door and padded through the house to greet Fawcett in the kitchen. In the pale morning light, the detective looked calmer than he had sounded on the phone—but only just.

"Good morning, sir," Fawcett began hastily. "I am sorry about the time."

Smalley forced a smile before turning his back. "This way," he said curtly. "And catch the door, will you?"

Fawcett followed his superior into the study, and they sat down facing each other in leather upholstered chairs. Smalley pushed a humidor toward his nervous guest.

"Cigar?"

Fawcett shook his head.

"No, thanks. I'm trying to quit . . . again."

"What's so urgent at. . . ." Smalley paused to consult a wall clock. ". . . Five-forty in the morning?"

"I think we got trouble," Fawcett said.

Smalley arched an iron-gray eyebrow.

"So you said on the phone, Jack. Can we have some specifics?"

"I don't know where to start, sir," the detective said. "Well . . . I mean, I don't even know *what* it means."

Smalley sighed resignedly, expelling a blue cloud of fragrant cigar smoke.

"Take your time, Jack. Try starting at the beginning."

Fawcett took a deep breath, held it an instant to steady his nerves, then let it go in a long, whistling sigh. The ritual complete, he began telling Smalley about the predawn shooting, his meeting and cryptic discussion with a man named La Mancha, and the subsequent discovery of three more leaking stiffs, exactly where the big stranger said they would be found. When he had finished, the two men regarded each other in silence for several moments through the haze from Smalley's cigar.

At last it was the commissioner who broke the silence.

"You believe there may be some connection between these killings and our other problem?"

Fawcett shrugged. "This guy, La Mancha, seems to think so, and he sure called it right on the second carload of meat. Frankly, I don't know *what* the hell to think."

"He's chasing the wind," Smalley said confidently. "What tie-in could there be, Jack?"

The lieutenant shook his head, obviously confused.

"I don't know, unless. . . . There has to be an angle, Chief. The feds wouldn't touch a sex crime case unless they thought they were onto something bigger."

"Bigger, Jack? What could they have?"

There was another long pause as the detective mulled that one over.

"If somebody's running his mouth overtime. . . ." he began.

Roger Smalley leaned forward, elbows on knees, jabbing his cigar toward Fawcett's face.

"Nobody knows, dammit," he said. "Nobody who's going to spill his guts, anyway. Everyone has too much to lose at this point."

"I suppose you're right, but . . . ."

Fawcett left the statement unfinished. He plainly was unconvinced.

"Go on," Smalley prodded.

"Well, Traynor suspects something," Fawcett said. "I know it."

The commissioner smiled patiently. "She's out of it, Jack. How many times must I tell you? Forget her."

"She could still hurt us," Fawcett countered.

"Relax, Lieutenant," Smalley said, making it sound like an order. "You're borrowing trouble. Leave the lady to me."

"What about the fed, this La Mancha character?"

Smalley shrugged.

"I'll ask around. In the meantime, play it cool and let me know if he contacts you again."

Fawcett nodded. "Sure, Chief. Okay."

"Is that other matter under control now?" Smalley asked.

"Huh? Oh, that. Yeah, I think so."

"You think so, Jack?"

Fawcett stiffened, hastening to make amends.

"Well, uh, I mean, the girl is still being stubborn, but the freeze is on. Anyway, what does she know?"

Smalley shrugged.

"She's a witness, right? She could get lucky."

Fawcett shook his head in a firm negative.

"No chance. I've had the identi-kit sketches recalled, and her verbal description could fit a couple thousand punks here in St. Paul alone."

"I hope you're right, Lieutenant."

The ice was back in Smalley's voice, unmistakable.

"I hold up my end," Fawcett countered. "You know that."

Smalley looked hard at him for a long moment, then visibly relaxed.

"Okay, I'll leave you to it. I have several calls to make."

"Are you going to bring the Man in on it?" Fawcett asked.

Smalley offered a thin smile to his subordinate.

"Why not? It's his mess, after all. If somebody has to sweat, who better?"

They shared a brief chuckle at that, and then Jack Fawcett rose to leave.

"Don't get up, Chief," he said quickly, when Smalley made no move to do so. "I can let myself out."

"Goodbye, Jack. And remember—*stay cool.*"

When Fawcett had gone, the commissioner snared the ornate telephone receiver from its cradle at his elbow. He listened to the droning dial tone for a long moment, thinking.

Fawcett was in a sweat, no doubt about that. Smalley didn't know yet whether his concern was justified, but he had every intention of playing it safe. The federal angle was a puzzler, and coming on top of the shootings that morning, it could mean trouble, but Roger Smalley was not about to panic before he had exhausted all logical possibilities.

He would make some calls. You didn't get to be the assistant P.C. in a city the size of St. Paul without making some high-level contacts at Justice. And if La Mancha—or whoever the hell he was— was working in Smalley's backyard, someone would know about it.

And finally, saving the best for last, he would call the Man.

Roger Smalley smiled at the thought, his first open, genuine smile of the day as he began dialing the telephone.

Hell yes, he told himself, there was already plenty of sweat to go around on that warm summer morning. And who better to do the sweating than the man who had started the whole frigging mess in the first place?

Roger Smalley's face froze in the smile. It was the grin of a predatory animal, carved in stone.

9

The scheduled meeting place was one of those plasticized restaurants, part of a chain, that always look and smell the same no matter where you find them. Bolan took a corner booth away from the broad front window and sat facing the doors. He was working on his first cup of mediocre coffee when Fran Traynor entered.

She glanced around the café, then spotted Bolan and crossed quickly to his booth. She slid in opposite him, and they sat quietly until a waitress delivered Fran's coffee.

She sipped at it and finally spoke.

"I've been thinking about what you said," she told him.

"What did you decide?"

She hesitated. "At first, nothing, but I wanted to keep digging on my own. Now...well...I'm thinking that you may be right."

Bolan was curious. "What changed your mind?"

Bolan noticed the slightest tremble in her hands as she set her cup down.

"After you left," she began, "I put through a call to a friend of mine on the rape squad. She really helped me get the unit started in the first place. She told me that all the eyewitness sketches of our Blancanales rape suspect have been withdrawn."

Bolan's frown was deep with anger.

"You have an idea who's behind this?"

The lady cop was nodding energetically.

"Jack Fawcett," she snapped, "it has to be. But I can't prove it right now. I know it sounds foolish. Women's intuition, and all that—"

"Not necessarily," Bolan said. "How much trouble would it be to have another sketch made?"

"No need," she said, flashing him a conspiratorial smile, and with a flourish she pulled a small rectangular card from her handbag, sliding it across the Formica table top to Bolan.

He examined the sketch closely, taking in the portrait of a long-faced young man, eyes set wide apart on either side of an aquiline nose, the mouth a narrow, almost lipless slit. The entire face was framed by hair worn fashionably long, hiding the ears.

There were no distinguishing marks or scars of any kind. Nothing to set that face apart from any of several thousand others on the streets of St. Paul and neighboring communities.

Bolan stared long and hard at the facsimile face, trying to see inside and behind it, to get a feel of its owner, but there was nothing there. The lifeless face stared blankly back at him.

Fran Traynor seemed to read his secret thoughts.

"Not a lot, is it?" she said.

"Not much."

"Except," she said, lowering her voice almost to a whisper, "I think I may have narrowed it down a bit."

Bolan stared at her.

"I have a friend on the unit who's been trying to call me since about the time you...that we went to the motel. The canvass of local sanitariums was completed last night ahead of schedule."

Bolan felt excitement growing in him.

"We have four possibilities," she revealed, "all of them committed to institutions within the past two years and escaped during the relevant periods."

"I wouldn't have thought that many." Bolan frowned.

"Wait a second," she continued. "We can narrow it further. One of the four is dead, and two others are back inside. That leaves one."

She looked pleased with herself. Fran sat back in the booth and drained her cup.

Bolan kept his tone deliberate and cautious.

"You're assuming the Blancanales rapist and your lady-killer are one and the same," he said. "But if that assumption is wrong, the two survivors still inside stay on the suspect list. Without a positive tie-in, either one could be your murderer."

Fran shook her head in a firm negative.

"No chance, La Mancha," she said stubbornly. "I know this is our man."

"All right, let's have it."

She gave him the recitation without consulting her notebook, holding his eyes with hers as she reeled off the facts from memory, chapter and verse.

"Courtney Gilman, age twenty-three, originally committed by his family two and a half years ago. That's soon after the first murder. He took a walk eleven months later—just before the second and third killings. Within a month he was back inside, for another eighteen months. He escaped again, and we had murders four and five before the family brought him back."

"Where is he now?" Bolan asked, certain he already knew the answer.

"Nobody knows," Fran told him. "He decked an attendant and hit the streets eleven days ago. That's one week before the attack on Toni Blancanales."

"Okay," Bolan said. "This does sound promising. But it's still from a circumstantial viewpoint. What would Fawcett or anyone else have to gain by covering for your suspect?"

The lady cop looked surprised at his question.

"What? Oh, of course, you wouldn't know. Courtney Gilman is the only child of Thomas Gilman."

She waited, expecting some reaction from the Executioner. It was not forthcoming. His blank expression told her that she wasn't making herself understood.

"Tom Gilman is a senior state legislator," she

said at last. "Street talk has it he may be our next governor. He's got all the marks."

"So we're talking about some sort of political arrangement," Bolan summarized.

"Possibly," Fran agreed. "Or blackmail—I don't know. At least it's an angle."

"It needs more checking, Fran. Where do I find this Gilman?"

"Gilman senior? Right here in St. Paul. I think he's originally from somewhere upstate, snow country. But we're the state capital here... where the action is, you know?

"He's worked his way up from councilman to the legislature, and the word is he won't be satisfied short of the statehouse. If his son is our man—"

"*If* he is," Bolan cautioned.

"Okay, right," the lady said, nodding. "Mr. Gilman could lose everything if the media pegged him as the father of a murdering maniac. He might try to make a deal...something...with Fawcett, or someone higher up."

Bolan thought for a moment.

"We're flying blind now," he said. "I need more than speculation before I hang the mark of the beast on a man."

"We can check it out," Fran insisted. "Confront Gilman."

Bolan shook his head.

"Not *we*, Fran. This is my game. You don't even know the rules."

She bristled at once. She fought to keep her voice down as she answered.

"I'm a police officer. This town is my territory, not yours. Who do you think—"

Bolan cut her off, quietly but firmly.

"You already suspect Fawcett, and if you're right, he couldn't run a scam like this alone. Who do you turn to?"

This time her response was hesitant, halting.

"I have friends on the rape squad. . . ."

"And if there is a cover-up, highly placed, they can't do any more than you can on your own," he finished for her. "Let it go, Fran."

Her face was set in an expression of grim determination.

"No way, buster. I'm not handing this over to you feds on a silver platter. The department can clean its own skirts."

"It's already been handed over," he said with finality. "I'm sorry, Fran, but you're out. Accept it."

Bolan sympathized with the lady, sure, and he let her know it.

"You've been of help," he offered. "Believe it. You can be of more."

"Name it."

"Teach me about rape," he said simply.

She looked at him, making no reply.

"What makes this headcase tick?" he continued. "I need to be inside his head, to see where he lives."

"Careful," she said, her voice softening, "it's dark in there."

"Why does he rape and kill?" Bolan prodded.

"Why not start fires, say, or rob gas stations? Why the sex angle?"

Fran leaned toward him, raising a slim index finger.

"Rape is a crime of *violence*, not sexuality," she said, secure, on familiar ground now. "Think of it as a personal assault, no different really from a shooting, or a beating."

Bolan nodded his awareness.

"But what comes *before* the fact?" he asked.

"Maybe rapists are inferiority complex types," she replied, "driven by the need to assert themselves and exercise control over a captive audience.

"That's one theory, anyway. That they perform not sexually, but emotionally. Each attack reaffirms their identity, makes them somebody to be reckoned with. For those few moments, they *exist*—they cannot be ignored."

"Do many rapists kill?"

"No. Maybe one in a thousand will deliberately kill his victim. We're dealing with a special breed of cat."

"A woman hater?"

"Possibly, but not necessarily. He probably hates everybody, and most of all himself. He ambushes women at night because he doesn't have the brains to build bombs or the nerve to climb a tower and shoot it out with the police."

"You read a lot from one sketch," Bolan said.

Fran smiled.

"Don't forget the M.O.," she said. "These

crimes are not only identical, they carry the killer's personality. With practice, you can read a crime like a signature.''

Bolan nodded. He understood that, sure, from the hard-won experience of his wars overseas and against the domestic Mafia cannibals. They left their marks, all right, like some sort of finger-print.

"Go on," he urged.

"Okay." She paused, collecting her thoughts. "This freak rapes his victims, and then he kills them with a knife. He mutilates them, but never sexually.''

"Explain, Fran.''

Another pause, and then she continued.

"Ninety-odd years ago, Jack the Ripper tried to shut down London's red light district single-handed. He never raped his victims, but he in-dulged in extensive mutilation. More often than not, sex organs were removed, and never found. Now, that is a sex fiend.''

"And our headcase is no Ripper?" Bolan asked.

Fran shook her head firmly.

"No way. Oh, superficially there's a similarity, sure. But our man stabs and hacks without any real direction, without any sexual aim. He de-faces his victims, diminishes them. And, thereby, he somehow enlarges himself.''

"Is he insane?"

She shrugged. "Medically? Of course. Legally, who knows?''

"What happens if he's arrested?"

"That depends. Of course, if there is some kind of plot to cover for him, he could be committed quietly—again. And he's already escaped three times."

"What if he goes to trial, Fran?"

"Maybe the same thing. A state hospital instead of some private institution, but those places have revolving doors. He could be 'cured' and released in a few years. Possibly months."

Bolan's voice was cool, determined.

"Okay," he said, "you've helped."

"That's it? End of lesson?"

He smiled. "School's out. And thanks."

"For what?"

"Some insight, some direction," he answered. "I can get inside him now."

When she spoke again, Fran Traynor's voice was almost pleading with him.

"They're not stupid, you know. Psychos, I mean. They get reckless sometimes, but underneath they're frequently as clever as they are vicious."

Bolan nodded. "Okay. I'll be careful."

He didn't need to be told how clever—and dangerous—a maniac with a self-imposed mission could be.

Bolan rested a warm hand on the lady cop's shoulder for a moment, left some change on the table for their coffees, then left her alone. As he hit the street in his rented sedan, the lady was already out of his mind, crowded from his thoughts by the multitude of things that remained to be done before the curtain could ring down on St. Paul's bloody stage.

First, he needed to touch base with the Politician and see what he had learned about the registration of the two crew wagons. He would have to follow that lead wherever it took him, before he could fit all the pieces together in their final mosaic.

And beyond that?

Somewhere out there, in the large city just stirring into life with the warming rays of the morning sun, there was waiting for him a young man with a blank face and a seriously deranged mind.

That young man, and perhaps several more besides, had an unscheduled appointment with the Executioner.

It was one appointment that Mack Bolan was grimly determined to keep.

10

Mack Bolan had come to St. Paul on what seemed a simple mission.

To help a friend.

To relieve the pain of a suffering comrade-in-arms.

But the nature of the Executioner's mission in the Twin Cities was rapidly shaping up into something else, something vastly different from what he had come to expect. The campaign had all the makings of a unique experience for Bolan in his home-front wars, and the very difference of the mission was what made it so desperate, so dangerous for all concerned.

For openers, Bolan had less solid information about his enemy—or enemies—than he had ever carried into battle before. In his previous campaigns, whether against the Cong, the Mafia, or the new breed of terrorists that John Phoenix had been resurrected to fight, he had always gone into combat with at least a general understanding of the enemy's number and goals.

He had always known their name and their game, yeah.

But not in St. Paul.

So far, the Executioner knew only that he was searching for one deranged young man who raped and murdered women for reasons best known to himself. An animal who had to be found and very forcefully neutralized.

But along the way, he had already encountered five men who bore all the earmarks of syndicate hardmen, and they seemed to be intent on scuttling any search for the Twin Cities rapist-killer.

That was a new one on Bolan, and he was a long way from having thought it completely through.

One thing was clear enough for the moment. He had come into St. Paul operating on faulty perceptions, without all the necessary information. Clearly, the game was not to be a simple, deadly one-on-one between the headcase and the Executioner. It had already evolved into something more, something larger, more sinister.

Someone had called out the guns in St. Paul; whether in support of Bolan's intended prey or on behalf of some unknown, unrelated cause, he couldn't yet be certain. He knew only that the gunmen existed, and that he undoubtedly would have to deal with more of them before he was finished in the city.

The strong indications of organized crime activity—and possible police complicity, whatever its scope—indicated that there was more at stake in St. Paul than a relatively simple string of rapes and murders committed by some faceless madman.

The Twin Cities had never ranked high in the American Mafia hierarchy, even before Mack the Bastard Bolan had appeared out of nowhere, rattling cages and finally blowing their whole damned house down. The syndicate had representatives and outposts there, nevertheless, and it carried out the same time-honored game of rape and ruin. However, the local action had never rated an Executioner visitation, either during the main war, or during Bolan's savage week-long "second mile" through hell.

Never, that is, until now.

Now it looked as if it might be time to correct an earlier oversight.

Across the nation, the crime syndicate lay in smoking ruins. But just as the V.C. had managed to avoid massive sweeps in Vietnam, just as the Japanese diehards had held out on isolated Pacific islands for decades after Hiroshima, there were still outposts and pockets of resistance that had weathered or entirely escaped the Executioner's cleansing fire.

And St. Paul, apparently, was one of those holdouts.

Syndicate chieftains had been reduced by the long Bolan blitz to the status of feudal warlords during the Dark Ages. Stripped of the seemingly omnipotent Mafia umbrella that had sheltered them for decades in America, they were now more cautious, more isolated from one another, more interested in perpetuating their local scams than in grand delusions of national power and prestige.

But that did not indicate any lessening of virulence at the local level. Hell, no.

Even a dying snake was dangerous if you came within reach of its fangs. And the Mafia viper, though hacked to pieces and scattered to the four winds, was still showing grim, reflexive signs of life.

At bottom, the stakes were—and always would be—basically the same for Mack Bolan. Civilized Man vs. Animal Man. The builders vs. the predators of the world.

From youth, Bolan had cast his lot with the civilized, the builders. Not that he had ever had any real choice in the matter. Given his upbringing, his sense of morality and duty, there was, quite simply, no option.

There had been no choice when he went to Vietnam to face Animal Man in the jungles of the delta, or when he reenlisted for a second tour of duty.

And there had been, yeah, no choice at all when the deaths of his parents and sister were laid at the doorstep of the malignant Mafia outpost in Pittsfield, so many lifetimes ago.

No choice, finally, when on the eve of victory in his Mafia wars, Bolan had been called to another front in the same war everlasting, to fight against worldwide terrorism as the reborn Colonel John Phoenix.

When Pol Blancanales called, seeking Bolan's help, there had been, again, no options for the Executioner. He had come to St. Paul because he had to, and if the enemy's number and name had been changed behind the scenes, that didn't alter his duty or devotion one iota. On the contrary.

Bolan would see his task through to the end, whatever that end might be, and he would strike against Animal Man with his last breath of life, if necessary.

There could be—hell, *would be*—no turning back short of victory or death.

And yeah, it looked like war everlasting all right. Mack Bolan vs. the cannibals in whatever twisted shape they might assume.

The Executioner knew he couldn't have it any other way.

11

A swift conversation with Pol Blancanales netted Bolan the information that the hardmen he'd encountered earlier that morning were driving vehicles registered in the name of Twin Cities Development, Inc. And the Politician's encyclopedic mind had filled in the fact that TCD was, in reality, a dummy corporation manufactured to front for the numbers and shylock operations of one Benny Copa, mobster.

Copa had been born Benjamin Coppacetti in the Hell's Kitchen district of New York City, and had migrated westward at the tender age of sixteen, one jump ahead of some heavy-duty robbery and assault indictments in the Big Apple. He had never been a real power in the Mafia, no one to be reckoned with outside St. Paul, even in the days before Mack Bolan's syndicate wars, but he was a localized underworld honcho of sorts.

He needed to know from Copa why the guns had been called out, and he needed that information before the day got any older.

Benny Copa operated from second-floor offices set above a billiard parlor two blocks over off Arcade Street. The place was called Freddy's, but there was no Freddy in residence, and no one in the neighborhood was quite sure anymore if he had ever existed.

Bolan found the place easily and parked his rental sedan a block past the darkened entrance, near an intersection. He had passed an alley as he circled the block, and he found it now on foot, moving cautiously along behind the businesses that faced the street. In a moment, he had reached the rear entrance of Freddy's.

And the place was locked. Naturally.

No pool hall would be open at that hour of the morning.

The cheap lock yielded quickly to the Executioner's pick, and he found himself inside a darkened doorway. The service stairs were immediately to his left.

Bolan's combat senses made a quick remote probe of the ground floor, picking up no sounds of human occupation. When he was satisfied that he wasn't leaving unknown dangers behind, he moved to the staircase, Beretta Belle in hand and ready to meet any challenge.

There was a hardman stationed at the top of the stairs, leaning back against the wall in a metal folding chair and dozing after a long night on duty. Bolan was almost on top of the guy when he woke, trying to right his leaning chair and reach holstered gunmetal in one awkward, unbalanced motion.

The Beretta coughed its single deadly word, and the guy went down with a thud, the chair rattling out from under him as he fell. His passing left a viscous crimson smear on the grimy wall.

Bolan had to assume that the racket of the hardman's dying had alerted everyone inside the adjacent office. He hit the door with a flying kick and burst in, the Belle up and seeking targets.

There were three of them, all clustered around a big desk littered with loose cash and crumpled bits of paper.

Three pairs of eyes locked onto Mack Bolan at his explosive entrance, noting his hard eyes and deadly side arm. Two of the men, conditioned by a lifetime in the mob's gutter wars, broke for their weapons, peeling off in opposite directions in an effort to divide Bolan's attention.

It almost worked.

But almost isn't good enough.

Bolan nailed the one on the left, plugging a 9mm mangler through the bridge of his nose before he could reach gun leather. Then he spun to take the guy on the right. Round one pinned the guy's gun hand to his chest as he was coming out of his death spin. Round two entered his gaping mouth and exited from the rear in a shower of blood and bone fragments.

And the sole survivor was taking it all in with astonished eyes, standing behind the desk with both hands flat on the broad top and making no move to leave it. His round eyes never left the smoking muzzle of Bolan's lethal Beretta.

Mack Bolan had known from the moment of

entry that this man would be Benny Copa, and that he would not be packing. The self-styled honchos of the mob considered themselves exempt from the dirty chores of the gun-bearers, and Bolan had learned from experience that that arrogance made them vulnerable in a pinch.

The pinch was on Benny Copa now, and he knew it.

Bolan crossed the office, his eyes and gun never wavering from Benny's pallid face. When he was less than a foot from the mobster, his Beretta almost grazing the little guy's nose and letting him savor the cordite smell of death, Bolan gave the guy a light push that dumped his slack form into a waiting swivel chair.

And at that, Benny Copa recovered enough of his voice to break the silence.

"Easy, man," he said, not quite pleading. "There must be some mistake."

"You made it, Benny."

Copa thought that one over quickly, licking dry lips.

"Well, hey, I mean...it can't be all that bad, can it?"

Bolan's face and voice were hard, unyielding.

"That depends on you."

And Bolan could see the guy's face and mind working, trying to read the possibility of a deal— or survival—into Bolan's words.

"Okay, yeah," he said at last. "I can dig it. Let's talk a deal here."

"Make it simple," Bolan said. "You have some

information, and I want it. You give, you live. Simple."

The look in Benny Copa's eyes was telling the Executioner that, yeah, the guy understood *simple* very well indeed. Copa nodded rapidly as he spoke.

"Fire away . . . hey, I mean . . . *ask*, okay?"

"You sent some crews out this morning, Benny. They didn't come home."

Copa's face registered shock at Bolan's inside knowledge. He covered it a second later, but not before Bolan had duly noted the reaction.

"Uh, I've got lots of crews, man," he said, stalling. "I run a big operation here."

"I'm only interested in two."

"Uh-huh, well . . . maybe we can make a deal here," he said, smiling craftily.

Bolan pressed the hot muzzle of the Beretta Belle against Benny's forehead, hearing the flesh sizzle on contact. He let Copa wince and wiggle for a moment before withdrawing the gun, leaving an angry red circle above the guy's left eye.

"You heard the deal, Benny. The minute I think you're shucking, I terminate the conversation."

And Bolan's tone left no doubt that the conversation would not be the only thing terminated, sure.

"Okay, okay," he said hastily. "Jesus, you can't blame a guy for trying."

"Sure I can," Bolan said.

Copa glowered back at his uninvited guest.

"Christ, you don't give a man much slack, do you?"

"The crews, Benny. Last chance."

"All right, dammit! We're talking about five boys, right? Two at the airport, and three more at a certain lady's house?"

Bolan nodded silently, letting the cornered weasel continue.

"Okay, right," Copa said, nodding affirmation of his own words. "They were part of a package deal. Outside contract, you know? Nothing to do with organization business."

And he smiled, as if that piece of information should settle everything.

But it didn't.

"What was their mission?" Bolan asked.

The little mobster managed a sarcastic snort.

"What do you think?"

The cold expression of the Executioner's face stifled the feeble snicker.

"They were disposal teams, man, you know?" Benny hastened to explain. "They were sent to dispose."

"Hit teams," Bolan said.

Copa nodded jerkily.

"Who was their mark at the airport?"

Copa shrugged elaborately, making a show of ignorance.

"Some dude, who knows? I told you it was an outside contract, right? The customer fingers his mark, and I count the dollar signs."

"I'll want the customer's name."

Benny Copa stiffened in his swivel chair, knuckles white as he gripped the armrests. There was new fear behind his eyes that had nothing to do with Bolan and the deadly silenced Beretta inches away from his nose.

The guy was silent for a long moment, but in the end the fear of clear and present danger won out, loosening his tongue.

"Really, man, I could buy real trouble by answering questions like that."

And it seemed the guy would never quit trying.

"You have trouble, Benny," Bolan reminded him curtly. "You're trying to buy time."

There was another, shorter pause. Then Copa opened up.

"Well, hey, I only know the dude's voice, can you dig it? We made the arrangements by phone."

Bolan's answering voice was almost sad.

"You commit five soldiers without knowing the customer's name? Goodbye, Benny."

The Beretta slid out to full extension, and Bolan was tightening into the final squeeze when Copa gave a strangled little yelp and threw out both hands, palms open, as if to ward off hurtling death.

"Wait! Shit! All right, man, I'm sorry."

The Beretta never wavered from its target.

"The name," Bolan said, his voice icy.

Benny Copa was sweating profusely. He wiped his forehead with a shirtsleeve, but it didn't seem to help.

"The name's Smalley," he almost whispered, "as in Roger. Satisfied?"

"What is he to you?" Bolan asked.

Copa looked incredulous at first, and then a canny little smile crept its way across his pale, damp face.

"You really don't know, do you?" Benny said, shaking his head. "I'll be goddamned and go to hell."

Bolan waited silently, ticking off the numbers in his head and staring at one round eye along the slide of his Beretta autoloader. Copa felt the vibrations of imminent death, and started talking again.

"Roger Smalley, man...he's only the deputy P.C. for all of St. Paul, that's all."

"So what was this Smalley character after? Why did he send you to the airport? No one knew I was coming in."

Now it was Copa's turn to be genuinely in the dark. "We weren't after you, man. All I know about you is what's going down now... And that's enough, thanks."

Bolan jammed the Brigadier's muzzle against the man's sweating nose. "Keep talking facts, little man. Who were you after? And why?"

"The customer said something about a bad detective," replied Copa, fast. "He said this dick had kidnapped a girl from the hospital. I guessed we had some sort of vigilante on our hands, a guy getting away with all kinds of shit and embarrassing the Commissioner. But it was just a contract, don't you see? No big deal."

Looking into Benny Copa's frightened eyes, he had no doubt the little guy was leveling with him.

He lowered the Beretta a notch, maybe half a notch.

"Okay, Benny," he said at last. "Live."

Bolan backed away from the littered desk and toward the door opposite. He could see relief tempered with caution flood into Benny Copa's face and form. The little mobster was desperately wanting—hell, *needing*—to believe that he was off the hook, but he couldn't quite accept it so suddenly. As the final realization hit him, he started to regain a touch of his natural bravado.

"Jesus, fella," he said, "you really had me going there."

After a quick glance around at the bodies on the floor, he added, "You also left me a helluva mess to clean up."

"Your problem, Benny," Bolan told him curtly. "You could have gone with them."

Copa snorted, grinning from ear to ear.

"Right, hell, buttons are everywhere . . . dime a dozen."

The little hood seemed struck by a sudden inspiration.

"Hey, wait," he called. "Maybe we can make another deal."

Bolan paused in the doorway.

"You've got nothing else I want, guy," he told the little cannibal.

"Well, Jesus, hear me out, huh? I'll double what you're getting now. Name your price. I could use a man of your . . . abilities."

Bolan said nothing. He was amazed at the guy's gall in trying to buy him and his gun.

"Listen, really," the mobster prodded, "I know natural talent when I see it. These boys were no shitheads, you know? Not like the old days, hell, but okay. You didn't take them out with no friggin' beginner's luck."

Bolan remained silent, letting the guy spill his guts.

"Fact is," Copa continued, "damned few guys I ever heard of could take two men...three men...in a face-to-face. Some of the old aces maybe, but hell...."

Behind those weasel eyes, wheels were turning, gears clicking into place as an embryonic idea or suspicion took shape. Benny's face underwent subtle changes, and Mack Bolan's gut rumbled in response, feeling something coming.

"You know, if it wasn't so goddamned far out...hey, uh, listen...that wouldn't be a Beretta you're holding, would it?"

Bolan saw the end coming, inexorably, the last unknown variables falling into place behind Benny Copa's suddenly haunted eyes.

And he nodded.

"You called it, Benny."

Copa's mouth worked soundlessly for a moment, then he licked his lips and tried again.

"You're dead, guy," was all he could manage.

"So are you," Bolan told him.

And the Beretta chugged once, putting a 9mm parabellum round through Benny Copa's left eye socket and slamming him over out of sight behind the desk. There was no need to check his condition, and Bolan didn't bother.

He put Copa's place behind him swiftly, his mind occupied with his own thoughts. As he reached the bottom of the stairs, the office phone began jangling overhead, loudly and insistently. There was no one up there to answer the call.

Back in his rental car and rolling, Bolan heard the grim words again in his mind. First spoken by Pol Blancanales in predawn darkness, and now, again, by the late and unlamented Benny Coppacetti.

You're supposed to be dead, guy. Dead and buried.

And yeah, theoretically, hypothetically, Mack Bolan was buried. Parts of him had been shed forever in Southeast Asia, in Pittsfield, in the final New York firestorm of his second mile against the Mafia.

It might come to pass that another part—or all of him—would be buried right there in St. Paul that very day, but he couldn't—hell, wouldn't—live in fear of the unknown and the inescapable. It was not his way, and never would be.

Mack Bolan was alive and living large.

All the way to a meeting with the assistant P.C. of St. Paul, yeah, and beyond that, if necessary, into the gates of hell itself.

12

From the journal of John Phoenix:

We live in a cyclical universe. It seems that everything repeats itself, and comes full circle given time. I know that to be true of life and death, love and hate. I am finding out that it is also true of war. Nothing stays the same in life or war, but in the end, nothing changes.

At one time, during one existence, the Mafia was my enemy and primary target. I believed that the disruption and destruction of their cannibalistic operations was the highest goal I could aspire to. With time, the "unwinnable" conflict resolved itself into something else, and I began to see a dim light at the end of the tunnel. And there was a victory of sorts, however temporary, but not before my war against the Mafia had gone full circle and returned to the city, to the ground where it had begun.

This is a new war, against new enemies, but I cannot escape a sense of *déjà vu*. The circles keep on turning, and in time all the faces of the predators and victims take on a similarity that is inescapable. I begin to feel that I am fighting the old war all over again, this time dressed up in a new disguise. The names of the enemies have changed, their addresses have shifted, but down deep, where the soul rot takes root and consumes healthy tissue, they remain the same.

Terrorism is the target this time out. But was it ever any different? At its most basic, stripped of all the political and religious window-dressing, terrorism is nothing more than a frontal assault upon the safety and security of the individual, or of society. It violates with a vengeance the most basic human rights of all: the rights to life and personal security. In the final analysis, it matters little if the victims of terrorism are held hostage in a foreign embassy, or cornered individually in the darkness of an underground garage. The end result, the violation of the person, is exactly the same.

It is that violation, that rape of the body and spirit, which we fight against. The enemy is always the same. Only the battlefield changes.

Terrorism is a time-honored concept, employed in one way or another since primal man learned to hide in the dark and leap out at unwary neighbors with his club. It would be fundamentally inaccurate to think that only certain groups, or particular segments of our population, perpetrate the crime. Terror has no color, language or religion; it is a universal constant, the writhing of a soul in fear and torment. At the bottom line, terrorism can only exist at an individual level, one-on-one.

The Mafia was expert at this kind of personal, one-on-one terrorism before its founding fathers stepped onto the dock at Ellis Island. Generations before the Palestinians or South Moluccans turned to violence in their different causes, home-grown terrorists were bleeding immigrant ghettos in America and sending out their tentacles into the everyday world of business and commerce. That terrorism was no less real, no less lethal, for being stripped of pseudo-idealistic songs and slogans. The victims were real, and the cost to America, in dollars and bloodshed, is undeniable by any thinking being.

It was that local terrorism that I set out to combat in the old war. I find now that I was only scratching at the surface, picking at a blemish while the cancer grew in size and strength just below the surface.

And things do come full circle. Wherever I go, however far I range away from the original battle-fields of my own private war, the echoes of that struggle call me back. The Mafia is like a fabled serpent, headless now, and hacked into pieces, but like the Hydra, each piece seems determined to grow a new head and put down deadly roots of its own. I expected that much when I charted my last mile against the Outfit, but I had hoped that it would take some time for the lethal new weeds to flower.

The time is now.

And terrorism, once again, has become very personal.

This one is for Toni, and for Pol. But it is also for myself, and for the other victims of a silent terrorism, past and present. Their blood cries out for vengeance, for a justice long denied them. If the war against the Mafia was unwinnable, quixotic, then this one against the violators can be little more than a localized delaying action. It may take a generation, and determined action by the courts and legislatures, to make our cities safe again for women—or for children, men, you name it. There is nothing that an Executioner can do to stem that tide of random rape and murder in our nation. A fighting man needs specific, individual targets, and just this once I have some.

I suppose it is the nature of the target that disturbs me. From the beginning of my home-front war against the mob, police have been untouchable to me. They are soldiers of the same side in a war against the creeping tide of lawlessness and violence that is terrorism at its most basic. I have met some cops—and some politicians, some lawyers, some doctors—who disgraced their oaths of office and their comrades by selling out to the very forces they are sworn to combat. I've been able to expose a few, and the reaction of their fellows in the field has been revulsion, the healthy body throwing off a contaminating parasite. In the end, with an occasional assist from outside, the lawmen have been both willing and able to police themselves.

And I have never fired on a policeman, or felt the urge to, before now. There were times, in that other war, when I could have eased my own way, or made the victory something more than partial, by taking out a cop. I do not believe you can defeat your enemy by *becoming* your enemy.

Sometimes, a man who is capable of bearing arms is faced with a positive duty to use those arms. At times, a man is duty-bound to kill so that others, the builders and civilizers, may go on about their tasks in peace. The predators must be held at bay, and there is no peaceful way to reason with the savages and cannibals among us.

But to kill a cop. . . .

The knowledge of a limited police complicity—however high-placed—comes as no surprise to me. I've seen too much of the corruption men are susceptible to. But for the first time, I may find it necessary to bend my own personal set of rules, to revise the guidelines of my war.

It is a new war, after all, at least in name. And it may require some new tactics, some new perspectives.

If Benny Copa and Fran Traynor are correct, then certain highly placed officials in this city have been aiding and abetting an insidious campaign of terrorism over months and years. It may well be impossible to build a solid case against them, or to find a prosecutor willing to attempt the job. In any case, the justice they deserve for wasting lives and violating souls will not be found in any courtroom. That justice must be swift, sure, irreversible. For Toni, and the others. For the universe.

And yes, it may be necessary to change some perspectives that I've carried for a lot of bloody miles. It may be time to face the fact that beyond a certain point, when he has passed some particular mile marker on the road of violence and corruption, even a lawman becomes hopeless, unsalvageable. He becomes a traitor, in the truest, most basic meaning of that hated term, and the penalty for treason is inescapable.

Before now, it has been something unthinkable, like spitting on the flag or changing sides in the middle of my own private war. The sides never change, but people do, and perhaps it's time for me to meet that fact head-on with respect to the targets I've acquired. Even flags, when torn and soiled beyond repair, are destroyed to make way for newer, cleaner ones.

So be it. I take nothing for granted in this struggle, and I keep an open mind with regard to targets and solutions. If it becomes necessary for me to take the final step, I will take it not with eagerness or anger, but with sadness—the quiet, personal grief that accompanies the death of an ideal.

And the war goes on, unchanged, unchanging. The target is still terrorism, whatever its face, name or position in society. And the victims, the souls hanging in the balance, are the same—the builders and seekers, the gentle civilizers. They are worth saving, worth protecting at any cost, and with that decision made, the other questions answer themselves.

The war goes on.

13

Assistant Police Commissioner Roger Smalley listened to the incessant ringing at the other end of the line, cursing softly to himself. After several long moments, he cradled the receiver, his mind racing to evaluate the ramifications of his problem.

Benny Copa would have to learn that he couldn't just waltz off to nowhere and leave a job unfinished. Especially this kind of job.

When Smalley had first heard from one of the metropolitan precincts that a girl, *the* girl, dammit, had been spirited out of hospital, he absolutely did not know what to make of it. And then the facts had started to come in. The girl belonged to some kind of detective agency. Able Company, or something like that. Another member of the agency was an out-of-towner, apparently her brother. And that stank. Smalley hadn't liked that at all. He wanted the stranger neutralized. That was Benny Copa's job.

And he blew it.

Not that Smalley now suspected Copa of running out on him entirely, oh, no. The little ferret didn't have the guts for that sort of double cross.

He was just irresponsible as hell, that was all, and more than a little uptight these days when it came down to getting his own hands dirty.

Smalley was considering ways to severely chastise Benny Copa if he couldn't raise him in the next half-hour, when the phone rang at his elbow. A little smile played across the assistant commissioner's face.

That would be Copa on the line, asking for instructions. The thin smile continued to play across Roger Smalley's lips at the thought of Benny Copa sweating it out, wondering what the hell was going on.

Smalley picked up the receiver on the third ring, taking his own sweet time about answering.

"Yes?"

"Hello? Commissioner Smalley?"

And it *wasn't* Benny Copa, dammit. Smalley couldn't place the female voice at the other end of the line.

"Speaking."

"This is Officer Traynor, sir. I'm sorry to bother you at this hour, but I . . . *we* have a problem that we need to discuss right away."

Smalley felt his throat muscles tightening, and he had to clear his throat before he could answer. He took a deep breath, telling himself that the woman sounded nervous and tired, and that he could undoubtedly control the situation if he only kept his cool.

And he knew what was coming, oh, yeah, only too well.

"Yes, Fran, what is it?"

Give them the old first name bit, and put them at ease. Make them think you remember them all and value them as individuals.

"Well...I...that is, I'm not really sure where to start."

Her confusion was obvious, and Smalley intended to turn it to his advantage from the start.

"The beginning?" he suggested amiably.

"Yes, sir," she said, sounding grateful, gathering her breath. And then she launched into a capsule recitation of the Blancanales rape case, her sudden transfer from the rape unit to public relations, her theory of the crimes and apparent proof of deliberate interference...and the sudden appearance of a big fed named La Mancha, out of Washington.

When Smalley had heard enough, he interrupted her.

"We don't want to discuss any more of this on the telephone. I'd like to meet with you in person, immediately."

She sounded immensely relieved as she answered, as if he had lifted the weight of the world from her shoulders.

"Yes, sir, whenever you say."

Smalley consulted the wall clock, thinking swiftly.

"We shouldn't be seen together at headquarters," he told her. "Assuming your suspicions are correct, we must take every precaution."

"Yes, sir."

He had her now. He could feel it through the wires.

"Very good," he said, stroking.

Smalley gave her a location and scheduled the meeting for thirty minutes later. They would discuss the details of Fran's suspicions at that time.

He put all the sympathy he could dredge up into his voice, gratified as her words fed back even greater relief and gratitude. Finally they ended the conversation with the lady thanking him profusely for listening, and he confirming that he would meet with her.

So far, so good.

Smalley had handled it well, and that knowledge almost dispelled the nagging tightness in his gut. Almost, but not quite.

Fran Traynor's call had been, among other things, a damned annoying interruption of his morning's plans. She had prevented him from placing his scheduled call to the Man, and now it would simply have to wait until he made some space, acquired more breathing room.

He tried Freddy's Pool Hall again, and slammed the phone down angrily on the seventh ring. Damn Benny Copa to hell, anyway.

Fishing a leather-bound address book out of a drawer in the end table beside him, Smalley riffled through the pages until he found a number accompanied only by cryptic initials. The old crocodile grin was pasted back on his face as he began dialing swiftly.

There were more ways than one to skin the proverbial cat, and more ways than one to get a dirty job done in St. Paul. Even on short notice.

Mack Bolan and Pol Blancanales sat together in the Executioner's rented sedan. The Politician had just finished wiring Bolan for sound, and a preliminary check of the tape deck on the seat between them proved that the miniature transceiver in Bolan's suit lapel was working perfectly. Pol seemed proud of his artistry.

"How's Toni holding up?" Bolan asked his old friend.

Pol forced a smile he didn't feel.

"I think she was glad to get rid of me for a while," he answered. "She's a trooper, Sarge, but she feels like she has to keep up some kind of a front . . . even around me."

Bolan nodded understanding. Toni could be like that, sure.

"She'll be fine, Pol," he said, recognizing the hollow ring of his words.

How the hell could he know the lady would be fine?

How the hell could anyone know that for sure?

Blancanales didn't seem disturbed. In fact, he seemed to appreciate the reassurance, and he tried to change the subject.

"How close are you?" he asked.

Bolan frowned, reading the hunger in his friend's eyes and hoping Pol could contain it there.

"Ask me again in an hour," he replied. "Right now it looks good, but it could go either way."

Blancanales shook his head grimly.

"It's hard to buy that about the assistant commissioner. The homicide guy, okay... but the damned commissioner?"

Bolan shrugged.

"Too many loose ends, Pol. I still need more before I can tie them together. My next stop may give me the pieces I need."

"I swear to God, Mack... if I thought the police were letting this happen... I...."

Pol broke off, his tone and expression anguished.

And there was anguish enough to go around, sure. For Toni, for himself, and for the ideal of justice he saw crumbling in front of his eyes.

"Not the police, Pol," Bolan reminded him gently. "One or two men, a handful at most. Men, buddy. You don't blame the orchard for a couple of bad apples."

"That's easy to say," Blancanales replied bitterly.

"It's the truth, and you know it. We've both met the Charlie Rickerts before. They don't take anything away from the best."

And yeah, the mention of Rickert's name brought grim memories flooding in upon both men as they sat there, bound together by a grievous common cause.

Charlie Rickert had been a bent cop, working on the Los Angeles force and taking payoffs from the mob in the early days of Mack Bolan's homefront war against the Mafia. And he had almost ended the Executioner's campaign single-handedly in the City of Angels—almost, sure, until another, honest cop named Carl Lyons had soured Rickert's play and let Bolan go with his life.

And both cops—the good and the bad—had left LAPD in the wake of the Executioner's strike in Southern California. Rickert had gone out in disgrace, banished to the netherworld of mob fringe activities, while Lyons had moved into the federal Sensitive Operations Group, assisting Bolan on several later campaigns.

Today, Charlie Rickert was dead, and Carl Lyons was a valued member of Able Team, one hard arm of Bolan's Phoenix operation in the war against international terrorism.

The good and the bad, yeah.

That was what the whole damned game was all about.

Pol Blancanales was nodding reluctantly. "I hear what you're saying, Sarge. But it's bitter."

And Bolan could accept that, too.

His own life had been bitter at times, and often. But it could be sweet, too, and he didn't want his long-time comrade-in-arms to forget that paramount rule of nature.

You go through the bitter to reach the sweet. Every time.

For a fleeting moment, the face of April Rose was locked onto Bolan's mental viewing screen, gradually transformed into the hunted, haunted countenance of Toni Blancanales.

The Executioner owed a supreme debt to both those ladies.

"You'd best get back to Toni," he told the Politician. "She can only stand so much solitude right now."

Blancanales nodded.

"Right, okay. I'll be manning the air and the landlines, buddy. If you need anything...anything at all...give a shout."

Bolan smiled warmly.

"Count on it."

They shook hands and then drove away in their separate cars, Pol returning home to his wounded sister, Bolan moving on toward a rendezvous with fate.

His fate, yeah. And, just maybe, someone else's.

The Executioner was going to drop in on a certain state legislator, and pass the time of day. Perhaps they would discuss the pains of friends... and family.

14

State legislator Thomas Gilman lived comfortably
in suburban West St. Paul, within an easy five-
minute drive of the fashionable Somerset Country
Club. Mack Bolan did a preliminary drive-by,
scanning the neighborhood for police cruisers or
suspicious vehicles, and found none.

On the second pass, he turned his rental car
boldly into Gilman's driveway and followed it
around to park directly in front of the big Dutch
colonial house. It looked as though politics had
been quite kind to Thomas Gilman.

Bolan rang the doorbell and listened to melodic
chimes sounding deep within the house. After several long moments, footsteps approached, and the
door was opened by a middle-aged man dressed in
vest and slacks without the matching jacket. His
hair was graying at the temples, and he regarded
Bolan with vague curiosity from behind wire-
rimmed spectacles.

"Yes?"

"Thomas Gilman?"

The man nodded, his curiosity deepening.

"Yes?" he repeated.

Bolan briefly flashed his federal ID in front of

the guy's face, pocketing it again before Gilman could focus on it clearly.

"Frank La Mancha, Justice Department," he said brusquely. "We need to talk."

Gilman raised an eyebrow.

"About what, may I ask?"

"Your son," the Executioner told him simply.

And it had the desired effect, yeah.

Tom Gilman paled underneath his professional sun-lamp tan, and for an instant Bolan watched him clutch at the ornate doorknob for support. Then the moment passed and Gilman regained control, stepping back to open the door and admit Bolan.

"Come in," he said, his tone formal, curt.

Bolan stepped into the entry hall, and Gilman closed the door behind him, leading the way to a combination library and study. He waved Bolan to a deep armchair and dropped into its mate nearby.

Bolan remained standing, hands in pockets, surveying the room and the man.

"When did you last see your son, Mr. Gilman?" he asked abruptly.

The politician's face showed mild confusion.

"Not in some time, why?"

Bolan countered with a question of his own.

"Was it before he escaped from the hospital?"

Gilman's face sagged, his whole body slumping as if Bolan had punched him hard over the heart. He plainly was stunned by the Executioner's words. His mouth worked silently for a moment; then he cleared his throat and tried again.

"I . . . I don't know what you're talking about,"
he offered lamely.

Bolan glowered at him.

"We don't have time to dance, Gilman," he
snapped. "I believe you know why I'm here."

A movement in the doorway caught Bolan's eye,
and he turned to find himself facing a woman of
indeterminate age, her curious eyes shifting back
and forth from Gilman to himself, and back again.

When she spoke, there was caution, even fear,
in her voice.

"Thomas, you haven't finished your breakfast."

Gilman waved her off with a distracted gesture.
"Not now, Louise, I'm busy."

The woman began to turn away, but Bolan's
voice stopped her on the threshold.

"Why don't you stay, Mrs. Gilman?"

She paused, looking again from her husband to
Bolan with narrowed eyes. At last Gilman nodded,
reluctantly, and beckoned her inside. She walked
past Mack Bolan to stand beside her husband's
chair, one hand resting on his shoulder.

"Louise," Gilman began, "this is Mr. . . . er. . . ."

"La Mancha," Bolan finished for him.

"Yes, quite. He's here about Courtney."

Conflicting emotions instantly twisted the
lady's face into a kaleidoscope of mingled hope
and horror. Bolan watched her fingers dig uncon-
sciously into her husband's shoulder, making him
wince.

"Have they found him?" she blurted. "Is he . . .
is he. . . ."

Gilman shook himself free, and snapped, "Louise! Control yourself!"

Bolan frowned at them both.

"He's still out there, Mrs. Gilman. I'm hoping you can help me find him."

There was a long pause as Gilman and his wife looked at each other searchingly. Finally, Gilman reached up to take hold of her hand, and she nodded to him, her eyes brimming with tears.

Gilman swallowed hard, and there was a catch in his voice as he began speaking.

"We don't know where he is. That's the truth. He...has no reason to trust us, Mr. La Mancha."

Bolan read the painful truth in Gilman's voice and saw the same hurt on the lady's face.

He believed the guy, yeah.

"All right. Let's start at the beginning."

Another soul-searching pause, and then Gilman resumed speaking, his voice broken.

"The beginning. How do you single out a point in time when you know your child is...*different*? Courtney was always a quiet boy. Introverted. Smart as a whip, but so damned quiet. Even as a child he could never open up or share his thoughts with us."

"He wasn't a *bad* child," Louise Gilman chimed in, sounding desperate.

Gilman gave her hand a gentle squeeze and continued.

"We both know what he was. What he is. By the time Courtney was six or seven years old, he had a violent, explosive temper. Not just the normal childish tantrums...there was real fury in him, deep down. He fought with classmates in grade school, and by high school he'd been in trouble several times. We changed his schools twice to protect him... from his own reputation."

"And to protect yourself?" Bolan asked, probing.

Gilman's head snapped up, eyes flaring angrily.

"No, sir!" he snapped, then the voice softened. "Not then. That all came... later. After...."

Gilman took a moment to compose himself and collect his disordered thoughts before continuing.

"In his senior year, a few weeks before graduation, there was...an incident. It involved a schoolgirl...a co-ed. There was some question of expulsion...of denying Courtney his diploma. I couldn't let that happen."

"So you pulled some strings," Bolan said. It wasn't a question.

Thomas Gilman nodded jerkily, and swallowed as if something had lodged itself in his throat.

"I have friends, Mr. La Mancha, connections. It is possible to arrange certain things. He was our child."

"And you had your own reputation to consider," Bolan added.

The suggestion didn't seem to anger Gilman this time.

"I don't honestly believe I thought of that...at that time," he said. "Subconsciously...who knows? Anyway, I promised to get help for Courtney, and we kept that promise. He spent eighteen months in analysis.''

"It didn't take," Bolan said.

Gilman nodded grimly.

"We realized that, in time . . . too late. It's always too late, isn't it?''

Bolan had no answer. He stood, watching the tortured couple in silence.

Gilman continued his narrative.

"Something over two years ago, there was . . . a murder. I paid no attention to it at the time. There were elections to win, and there was legislation to pass. Courtney was staying out all night, every night, doing who knows what.

"Anyway, one night he was arrested . . . as a prowler, I think. Apparently he broke down under questioning and . . . he confessed . . . to rape and murder.''

The final words were almost strangled, coming out in a barely audible whisper. Beside Gilman, his wife turned away, stifling a sob with one hand.

Mack Bolan was starting to get the picture.

"You got a phone call," he offered, certain what the answer would be.

Tom Gilman nodded, unable to meet Bolan's gaze as he shifted his hands nervously in his lap.

"From a lieutenant named Fawcett?" Bolan pressed, seeking the final raw nerve that would release the last of the story.

Gilman looked up quickly at that, his expression one of confusion.

"Who? No, I don't recognize the name. I was

called by Assistant Commissioner Smalley. Of course, he was only a deputy chief at the time."

Bolan concealed his surprise at the name. Things were beginning to fit. Only too well.

"What did Smalley have in mind?"

Gilman flashed a bitter, sardonic grin.

"Oh, nothing complicated," he said. "A sort of symbiosis. Mutual back scratching. He would guarantee 'fair treatment' for Courtney, and I would be. . .properly grateful."

"Your son's confession was misplaced?"

Gilman spread his hands.

"Presumably. Filed away for future reference, I suppose. At the time, I wasn't interested in the mechanics, only results. Smalley was. . .effective. The prowler charge was quietly dismissed, and we placed our son in a suitable institution."

"How did he escape?"

Gilman shrugged listlessly.

"No one seems to know, or at least they won't admit it. The hospital wasn't designed for maximum security."

Bolan saw no need to dwell upon the murders that had followed Courtney Gilman's first escape. . .or his second. The Executioner had heard enough about the lax security in even the best mental hospitals to know that escapes were commonplace. The Boston Strangler, for one, had made a habit of leaving his padded room behind to kill, returning when he was finished, and no one had been the wiser until he confessed, probably from sheer boredom and frustration.

In any case, Bolan was more interested in the mechanics of the cover-up than in the details of murder.

"How was he recaptured?" Bolan asked.

Gilman still wore the bitter smile.

"Smalley has his ways, I suppose. He keeps the details to himself, but he made sure we realized that Courtney had... been in trouble again."

And, yeah, Bolan could see the pattern clearly now. The mad youth escaping, killing, being recaptured—probably by Jack Fawcett—returned to the sanitarium, only to escape and kill again. And again. And with each new crime, each new escape, Tom Gilman's complicity increased, Roger Smalley's blackmail hold was strengthened.

Gilman's taut voice interrupted the Executioner's train of thought.

"I made Smalley, you know," he was saying. "At least, I helped put him where he is. A nudge here, a word there. I was properly grateful, oh, yes."

Bolan read a bitterness approaching self-hatred in the politician's voice.

"Five lives!" Gilman said, almost sobbing. "Five young women dead. Oh, I'm well aware of my achievements, Mr. La Mancha."

Bolan's frown deepened.

"There's guilt enough to go around, Gilman," he said soberly. "Sort it out later. Right now, I need your help. Your son's sixth victim needs help."

Louise Gilman let out a strangled gasp. "A sixth? Dear God!"

"A survivor," Bolan said. "The next may not be so lucky."

Gilman's answering voice was a plea for belief and understanding.

"I swear we don't know where he is. He blames us for locking him away, you see. Our son is logical, if nothing else. He wouldn't contact us if his life depended on it."

"It might," Bolan told him.

Man and wife looked at him long and soulfully. Bolan was certain they had nothing more to tell him. He was ready to disengage when Gilman broke the tortured silence.

"How . . . how did you find out about our son?" he asked.

Bolan sensed the deep anxiety, a continuing terror, beneath the words.

"It's not common knowledge," he replied. "Not yet. But the numbers are running out, Gilman."

Gilman nodded resignedly.

"I've been expecting it for some time. Maybe hoping for it, secretly—who knows? I plan to make a clean breast of everything this afternoon at a press conference."

Bolan's brow furrowed; his mind raced ahead.

"I hope you'll reconsider that," he said earnestly, "at least until you hear from me again."

"But why?" Gilman looked honestly confused now. "If I can warn one person . . . save even one life . . . ."

"It's too late for noble gestures now," Bolan said curtly. "Save your story for the courtroom, where it will have some real impact."

The Gilmans were thinking that over as Bolan turned to leave them. He paused in the doorway, half turning.

"I'll be in touch," he told them both. "If you hear from your son in the meantime—"

"I can handle it," Thomas Gilman assured him.

There was infinite sadness in the older man's voice, and yeah, Mack Bolan believed that the guy would be able to handle it if it happened.

He left them alone with their mutual grief and let himself out of the house. Back in his car, he punched the rewind button on the cassette tape deck, recycling a portion of the tape, which was almost used up. When he had reached the mid-point of the reel, he hit the play button.

The taut, anguished voice of politician Thomas Gilman filled the rented sedan.

"It's always too late, isn't it?"

Bolan silenced the tape and started his car. He was releasing the emergency brake when the little radio transceiver on the seat beside him clamored for attention.

"Stony Man...Able One calling Stony Man.... Come in!"

Bolan snared the radio and answered.

"Stony Man. I read you, Able."

Even on the airwaves, Pol Blancanales sounded desperate.

"Toni's gone, Sarge," he gasped. "I...when I

got back, the place was a mess. She's been kidnapped."

Bolan felt his guts tying themselves into the old, familiar knots.

"Any leads, Able?"

"Negative, dammit! Another two minutes, and...oh, Jesus!"

"Easy, Able. The lady needs you in one piece, so hold it together."

And yeah, he could almost visualize his friend straightening up, stiffening at the other end of the connection.

"Right, you're right," Blancanales answered after a moment. "What do we do?"

"Stay put, Able," Bolan told him. "I have one more base to touch before we connect. Have you called the police?"

"Negative. All I could think of was getting in touch with you."

"Roger, Able. I'll make the contact myself. Out."

Bolan dropped the silent radio onto the seat beside him and put the car in roaring motion. As he headed back toward downtown St. Paul, the words of Thomas Gilman came back again to haunt him.

It's always too late, isn't it?

Bolan clenched his teeth, hands tight on the steering wheel.

For the sake of everyone involved, he devoutly hoped that Gilman was wrong on that score.

15

Roger Smalley parked his Cadillac on the southern boundary of Calvary Cemetery, along an unpaved access road sandwiched between a Cyclone fence and a set of railroad tracks. Beyond the fence, headstones and crosses marched away in solemn diagonal ranks.

He had been waiting five minutes or so when Fran Traynor's foreign compact car turned onto the access road and pulled up behind him. The dust took a moment to settle, and then she left her car, moving around to slide in on the passenger side of the Caddy.

"Good morning, sir," she offered, smiling faintly. "I'm really sorry about all this."

Smalley returned the smile, waving her apology away.

"Nonsense. If you're correct in your suspicions, I want to get to the bottom of it immediately." He watched her relax visibly. "Now, why don't you start at the beginning."

The lady cop took several moments to put her thoughts in order, and then she began speaking in hushed, hurried tones.

"I'm convinced that Lieutenant Fawcett is suppressing evidence in a multiple rape-murder case. He's withdrawn all the suspect sketches without explanation. He's done everything possible to discredit the only real witness, he—"

Roger Smalley raised a hand to dam the sudden flow of words.

"All right, take it easy. On the telephone you mentioned a suspect."

Fran Traynor nodded excitedly.

"Yes, sir, that's the clincher. It turned up in a routine check on the local sanitariums."

And the assistant police commissioner of St. Paul sat there listening, while the attractive lady cop laid out the whole circumstantial case against one Courtney Gilman. He heard it all, feeling the old familiar tightness and burning in his stomach, keeping one eye riveted to the rearview mirror.

Fran was just finishing her presentation, her excited voice winding down, when a black car turned onto the gravel access road, closing the exit behind her compact. The doors on either side opened, disgorging several men in dark suits.

As Fran Traynor finished, Smalley idly unbuttoned his suit jacket, sliding a hand inside to encircle the butt of his holstered .38.

"I believe you may be on to something, Traynor," he said, smiling at her.

The lady cop started to answer that smile with a relieved one of her own, but it vanished as she saw the revolver in Smalley's hand, its squat muzzle aimed directly at her chest.

Smalley broadened his grin, feeling better now.

"Now, if you'll hand over your purse...."

Instead, she flung it at him, aiming for his face, twisting away at the same instant and clawing for the interior door handle. Smalley batted the handbag aside and clubbed her hard behind the ear with his revolver. Her forehead smacked against the window glass, and she gave a stifled yelp as she rebounded, landing prostrate and unconscious with her head resting on the commissioner's thigh.

At that moment the passenger door of the Cadillac was opened, and one of the new arrivals leaned in, letting appreciative eyes wander over the provocative display of leg where Fran's skirt had hiked up during the struggle. He flashed Smalley a lecherous grin.

"Not bad, Commissioner," he chuckled.

Smalley's mouth turned down in distaste. This one was worse than Benny Copa.

"Put a lid on that," he snapped curtly. "You're here to do a job, nothing else."

The hardman lost his smile.

"Yeah, sure. We hold her with the other one until we hear from you."

Smalley nodded.

"Right. It shouldn't be more than an hour or two at the most."

"Okay." The man nodded.

He edged over to accommodate a second burly figure in the doorway, and together they leaned into the Caddy, hauling Fran Traynor outside and letting the skirt bunch up around her hips in the process. Roger Smalley heard the evil snicker again and turned away in disgust, closing his mind to it, waiting until the door clicked firmly shut.

He was alone once more.

The assistant police commissioner fired the Caddy's power plant and pulled away, avoiding the rearview mirror with his eyes. There was a sour taste in his mouth, as there always was when he was forced, at this stage of his life, to deal with scum. But he knew from grim experience that the human savages and garbage of the earth could have their uses . . . so long as they were firmly and strictly controlled.

Smalley was glad to be leaving them behind. And, at least temporarily, to be leaving his problems in their hands.

It seemed fitting, somehow. The dregs of the earth helping a basically decent man salvage his life and his career. Keeping him in the position he had clawed and fought for over the past fifteen years.

Not that the struggle had been so great since Jack Fawcett discovered Courtney Gilman, oh, no. But the nagging pain in his gut was the same, if not worse. And the worries were still there, damn right, in abundance.

Now Roger Smalley had a plan for eradicating those problems once and for all, without giving up any of his gains. It would require a modicum of luck, sure, but Smalley was feeling lucky that morning. Batting a thousand in the problems department.

And with luck, he might soon be free of the whole stinking Gilman dilemma.

Roger Smalley smiled to himself as his vehicle rolled onto pavement again and he nosed it back in the direction of his office.

Fran Traynor and her big, loose mouth were in the bag, and they were going to stay there. Damn right.

And the commissioner's problems were already starting to fade like the memory of a half-forgotten nightmare.

16

Lieutenant Jack Fawcett entered his office reluctantly. He had things on his mind, and he wasn't looking forward to writing up the dead-body reports on five cooling stiffs, not with all the other things he had to think about.

Damn Roger Smalley, anyway. And damn *himself*, for ever hesitating when the Gilman kid started spilling his guts down in interrogation room number four. Why in the hell had he ever thought of calling the commissioner—deputy chief then, he reminded himself sourly—to ask for advice on the case?

"Advice" my ass, he thought grimly.

He had seen a ticket to the gravy train, sure, and he'd put through the call to Smalley on the off chance that a hint in the right place might put him on board for a nice long ride.

It had turned out to be more like a one-way ticket to hell. At least for Jack Fawcett.

Smalley didn't have any complaints, of course. He was sitting up there next door to the commissioner's office and smoking his fat cigars without a single worry. Smalley had the world in his pocket, while Detective Lieutenant Jack Fawcett spent his days and nights wading in the sewer of man's violence. Smalley went to banquets while Fawcett went to autopsies, staring at rigid corpses under cruel fluorescent lights.

Five corpses in particular.

All of them under thirty, all female, all once attractive but bearing the trademark of an animal who mauled them and mutilated them, casting them aside like so much garbage in the street.

The first one of the five was free, okay. That one had been out of Fawcett's hands, beyond his control. But the other four....

He felt their ephemeral weight on his soul.

He knew, deep down where it mattered, that they were dead because of *him*, as much as because of the freaked-out psycho who wielded the knife.

The nightmares had started again, around the time of the Blancanales rape. Fawcett had thought, foolishly, that he was rid of them, but now he knew better. They were back to stay.

Each dream was the same—or almost. Each time he imagined himself at home, asleep in his own bed, when he was roused by a strange, indescribable sound outside the window. He would rise, picking up his service .38 from the bedside table, and pad softly to the window, peering outside into midnight darkness.

And the girls were always there. Pale and rigid, eyes locked open in death, crusty stains upon their fluttering shrouds. And each one held an arm outstretched, accusing fingers pointed

straight at *him*, for Christ's sake, while they
moaned and wailed their wordless accusations
through pale, pale lips.

There had been one girl in the first dream.

Now there were four.

Jack Fawcett wondered how many his front
yard could hold.

He flopped down in his office chair, and for the
first time his eyes caught the note lying on top of
his desk. He recognized the spidery handwriting
of the dick on the graveyard shift, and he held the
note close, reading slowly.

It said, simply: "Jack—Call Pinky."

Okay.

"Pinky" was one of several street snitches who
served Jack Fawcett on a semiregular basis. As
every working detective knew, the majority of
cases could never be solved by the old Sherlock
Holmes routine. You needed a good, reliable
pigeon to finger your suspect and drop the case in
your lap when the going got tough. Then a good
cop could keep up his record, and the snitch could
be happy with whatever crumbs were passed
down the chain of command.

This particulr snitch was a junkie, one of those
burned-out zeroes who used to be called bums and
dope fiends but how had been rechristened
"street people" sometime during the late sixties.
Fawcett had busted him once, long ago, deciding
on a hunch to let him slide in return for a larger
bust, his supplier. Pinky had come through with a
righteous bust, and it had only cost Fawcett a tiny
piece of the dealer's stash.

A good deal, yeah, although the details had made a younger Jack Fawcett slightly nervous in retrospect. Since the first time, he had dealt with his snitches strictly on a cash-and-carry basis.

Lately, Pinky had put Fawcett on to a couple of pretty good busts: a mugger who liked to go all the way with his marks, and a pair of Oklahoma cowboys with a penchant for stick-ups and a no-witness policy. Most recently, Fawcett's snitch had been keeping his ear to the street, seeking any rumbles on the possible whereabouts of a young man named Courtney Gilman.

Fawcett dialed a number from memory, and a familiar voice answered on the fourth ring.

"Yeah?"

The snitch sounded sleepy or drugged. Probably some of each at that hour of the morning.

"I got your message, Pink. What's shakin'?"

Fawcett could hear his informer coming alive and alert at the other end of the line.

"Oh, hey, right, man. I knew you'd want to hear it right away. I tried your home number, but—"

Fawcett interrupted him brusquely.

"Hear what, Pinky?"

"Huh? Oh, yeah, man, I'm pretty sure I got your pigeon."

Jack Fawcett tensed, craning forward in his chair and gripping the telephone receiver in a stranglehold. His knuckles whitened.

"I'm listening," he snapped.

Pinky gave him the address of a cheap fly-by-night hotel not far from Riverside Park, and the number of the room where his suspect was last registered. Fawcett noted the address and number on a scrap of paper and pocketed it.

"If this pays off, I owe you one, Pinky," he said.

The drugged voice cooed back at him.

"Okay, man. This is the real skinny, no shit. I wouldn't shine you on."

"You'd better not."

The guy's voice took on a new tinge, that of fear.

"No sweat, man, it's straight."

"Okay."

Fawcett hung up and hurried downstairs to his cruiser. The drive to the fleabag hotel took him twenty-five minutes, and he cursed every red and amber traffic light on the way.

The detective parked in a red zone next to a fire hydrant and went inside, unbuttoning his jacket on the way to make his holstered .38 more readily accessible. Inside the dump, a sallow-faced desk clerk laid his body-builder magazine aside and leaned across the registration desk on scrawny arms.

Fawcett knew at once that the guy had made him as a cop.

"What can I do for you, officer?"

The sneer was barely concealed in his voice. Just well enough to avoid the certainty of loosened teeth.

Fawcett scowled, marking the bum down as a smart-ass.

"Who've you got in number twenty-six?" he demanded.

The desk clerk spread his hands.

"I ain't the nosy type. Anyway, I just came on at six."

"Let's check the register, shall we?"

The clerk feigned shock at the suggestion.

"Ain't that an invasion of privacy or somethin'?" he asked, wide-eyed.

Jack Fawcett flashed a disarming smile, then reached quickly over the desk to snare a handful of the guy's fishnet shirt, half dragging him across until their faces almost touched. The detective's smile was gone, and his free hand held a stubby blackjack, lightly stroking the thick leather across one of the desk clerk's pallid cheeks.

"I didn't quite hear you, scumbag."

The guy was shaking, suddenly anxious to please.

"The register, sure, right away," he gasped, sucking air like a fish out of water.

Fawcett shoved him roughly backward, and the guy took a second to recover his balance, then produced a battered ledger from beneath the counter. He thumbed through several pages, paused, and read aloud.

"Tha—that'll be a male single, man. Gave his name to the night clerk as Joseph Smith."

It was Fawcett's turn to sneer. "How original."

The guy considered a reply, but thought better of it. He shrugged.

"He in?" Fawcett asked.

Another shrug.

"No idea, man. Probably, this early, but who knows?"

"You got phones in the rooms?"

The clerk shook his head jerkily.

"Naw, just a pay job on the second and fourth floors. Your man's on the second."

Fawcett aimed a warning finger at the guy's face, pistollike.

"Let's make sure that phone doesn't ring, eh?"

As he stowed the blackjack in a pocket, he let his jacket flare open to reveal the holstered revolver at his waist.

Jack Fawcett took the dirty steps two at a time, bypassing the ancient elevator. Upstairs, a murky hallway carried the pervasive odors of age and accumulated filth.

He paced off the hallway until he stood before the door to room twenty-six. Gingerly he tried the knob and, of course, found it locked.

Damn.

It had been a long shot, anyway.

Fawcett drew his .38 and thumbed the hammer back. He took a short step backward, then hit the door with a flying kick just beside the lock. There was a sound of splintering wood as the ancient door exploded inward.

Fawcett charged into a small, half-darkened room. Greasy curtains admitted dappled light, producing surrealistic nightmare shadows. Directly across the room, a slender figure was coming suddenly awake, thrashing around in tangled bedsheets.

Jack Fawcett rushed to the bed and with one hand shoved the boy flat on his back, leveling his pistol at the upturned face. Familiar young-old eyes stared up at him with a mixture of fear and hatred. They were wild, animal eyes.

For an instant, the detective was overwhelmed by the temptation to squeeze the trigger of his .38 special and be done with it forever. His finger was tensing into the pull, his eyes narrowing, when he came to himself and shook the moment aside.

His voice was bitter, savage.

"Surprise, asshole. Flip over and assume the position."

Courtney Gilman did as he was told, rolling over and bringing clenched fists around behind his back. Fawcett cuffed them there, then used his spare set of handcuffs to shackle one of the boy's slender ankles to the bed frame.

The young man lay before him unmoving, silent. His entire being seemed to radiate an insolence—an evil—and once more Fawcett felt his hand tightening involuntarily around the .38. He controlled himself with an act of will.

Jack Fawcett knew what he had to do, what duty and circumstance demanded. He left the room, leaving the door ajar, and moved swiftly to the pay telephone at the near end of the corridor. He dropped a dime into the box and dialed the number of Roger Smalley's office.

Fawcett was surprised to note that his hands were trembling.

A secretary took his call and patched him

through to the assistant commissioner. In a moment, Smalley's curt voice filled his ear.

"What can I do for you, Jack?"

"It's what I can do for you, Commissioner," he said, resenting the man's haughty tone. "I've just taken delivery on that package you wanted. It's ready to be passed on."

Smalley's voice brightened instantly, losing its curt tone and becoming cheerful.

"That's excellent news, Jack, excellent. I couldn't be happier."

Fawcett felt something out of place in the man's tone, but he couldn't put his finger on it.

"Where, uh, should I deliver the goods?"

Smalley cleared his throat softly, hesitating.

"We've had a change of plans today," he answered at last. "Something unexpected. I'm going to have to meet you personally on this."

Fawcett's mind was filled with the sudden jangling of alarm bells. He felt the short hairs on the nape of his neck standing at attention.

And he remained silent, waiting for Smalley to continue.

"Jack? Are you there?"

Where the hell else would he be?

"Yes, sir, right here."

"I'm going to take delivery in Phalen Park, Jack. Follow West Shore Drive, and I'll meet you by the water. Give me forty-five minutes."

"All right. Whatever you say."

Smalley detected his nervousness, and the commissioner sounded concerned.

"Is there any problem with that, Jack?"

Fawcett's answer was hasty as he tried to cover his feelings.

"No, sir, no problem. I'll be there with the package."

Smalley's voice smiled back at him.

"Excellent. Goodbye, Jack. And thank you."

Fawcett listened to the buzzing dial tone for a full minute before hanging up. His mind was racing, trying to anticipate Smalley's plan, and coming up short each time.

Clearly, the guy had something up his sleeve, and whatever the hell it was, it could spell trouble. Jack Fawcett knew Smalley well enough by now to be suspicious of him. He only wished he had possessed such intimate knowledge before he placed that very first call to the commissioner concerning Courtney Gilman.

Spilt milk, he told himself gruffly. No use crying.

He would keep his appointment with Smalley, there was really no choice in the matter. But he wasn't walking into it with his eyes closed either.

The assistant P.C. wasn't going to make a monkey out of Detective Lieutenant Jack Fawcett. Not a monkey, or a scapegoat. Or a corpse.

The change of plans could only mean unexpected trouble, and Fawcett knew in advance that Smalley would try to shake off as much of the shit as he could, to dump it on somebody else.

And Jack Fawcett didn't intend to make himself a handy target.

It would all be so easy. Go back into that

damned dingy room and unlock the handcuffs that held Courtney Gilman to the bed like a hobbled calf. Back off a few paces, and *bam!* One psycho in the bag.

So easy, yeah. And so impossible.

Jack Fawcett had chosen the path himself, with a phone call long ago. Now he had no choice but to follow the path he had set, and try, just try, to have some say in the way it ended up.

Cursing, the detective stalked back down the hallway to collect his prisoner.

17

For Assistant Commissioner Roger Smalley, it had been a day dominated by telephones. First, the wake-up call from Jack Fawcett had promised to ruin the day entirely, and then the second interruption from Fran Traynor, had sent his ulcers into angry, growling protest.

The telephone had even conspired to vex him in its silence, refusing to connect him with Benny Copa when he needed the goddamned hoodlum most.

Only the last call, again from Jack Fawcett, had promised relief from a day fraught with potential disasters. Maybe, just maybe, the pieces were starting to fall into place.

Smalley could proceed with his plan now, full speed ahead. And the added embellishment promised by Fawcett would tie the whole thing up into one bright, shiny package.

An early Christmas present, sure. Why not?

But the damned telephone was ringing again!

Smalley punched a button to answer the interior office line, and his secretary's sultry voice issued from the speaker at his elbow.

"I'm sorry, Commissioner, but there's a Mr. La

Mancha on line one, calling from the Justice Department."

La Mancha.

Smalley went cold for an instant, his hands clenched into fists on the desk top. Then he forced himself to relax, inch by inch.

"Thank you, Vicky," he said, pleased to find his voice in perfect control. "Put him on, please."

There was a click, and a moment of dead air followed by a humming sound, then Smalley sensed another presence on the line.

"Assistant Commissioner Smalley here," he said jovially. "Can I help you?"

"I wouldn't be surprised."

It was a deep voice, firm and strong. Knowing, somehow. You could read a million things into that suggestive intonation. Smalley fought to keep his imagination from running away with him. How much could the damned guy know, after all?

"Is there something St. Paul can do for the department?" Smalley asked.

La Mancha's answering tone was curt.

"Forget the department, guy. I just had a chat with Thomas Gilman about his family problem."

Smalley stiffened in his chair, fighting the involuntary tremor in his limbs. He forced his voice to remain strong and even.

"What? I'm afraid I don't know what you're talking about."

"I'm talking about Thomas Gilman. I believe you know him—and his son—very well."

Smalley felt as if his world was about to col-

lapse around his ringing ears. He gulped a deep
breath and held it for an instant, letting it out
slowly as he fought to marshal his thoughts, to
control the painful rumbling in his gut.

"I'd like to know who I'm talking to," he said at
last. "If you're not with Justice—"

La Mancha cut him off again.

"Spell it with a small *J*. And the who doesn't
matter, compared to the *what*."

Smalley was growing more and more confused.

"Well, then. . . ."

"We're talking about murder, Commissioner,
times five. And the one who got away."

Smalley tried to put the man off, stalling for
time.

"It sounds like you want our homicide division,
Mr. La Mancha. I could give you the number."

"I've already spoken to homicide," the caller
told him simply. "My next call goes to the media."

"What?"

It was as if an invisible fist was clenched
around Smalley's vocal cords, and he cursed his
own lack of control.

The stranger's answer chilled him to the bone.

"I have a tape here with me that the city editors
should be interested in," he said.

Smalley's mind was filled with a crush of conflicting, near-hysterical thoughts and fears. A
tape? From Gilman? Had the yellow son of a bitch
broken down and spilled his guts to a G-man, for
God's sake?

No, La Mancha had already indicated he

wasn't with the department. Okay. A blackmailer could be handled, paid off in more ways than one.

"Perhaps, uh, if you filled me in on the details...."

Before Smalley could finish the sentence, he heard the hissing sound of a tape in motion, and over all the sound of two familiar voices.

One voice belonged to his caller, the man named La Mancha.

The other belonged to Thomas Gilman.

"...broke down under questioning and...he confessed...to rape and murder."

"You got a phone call."

Silence. Smalley could picture Gilman's head bobbing in assent.

"From a lieutenant named Fawcett?"

"Who? No, I don't recognize the name. I was called by Assistant Commiss—"

Mercifully, the tape ended, cut off in mid-syllable.

Roger Smalley sat dumbly in his chair, feeling numb, shaken to the very fiber of his being. For an instant he almost panicked at the thought of those recorded words coming over an open line, but he calmed himself. No one could tap his phone without his learning about it in short order. He was the Assistant Police Commissioner, for Christ's sake!

The voice of the man called La Mancha was back on the line, demanding Smalley's attention, calling him out of himself.

"Heard enough, Commissioner?"

There was, surprisingly, no mocking tone in the words. The man seemed almost...well, almost sad, somehow.

Smalley's answering voice was low, taut.

"What is it that you want?"

La Mancha's answer came back at him without hesitation.

"Toni Blancanales, safe and sound."

And that was all.

Smalley risked everything on another stall.

"What makes you think—"

He never got it out. La Mancha's voice was a razor slicing across his words, terminating them in mid-sentence.

"I also had a talk with Benny Copa. He was cooperative to the last." Smalley's mind flashed back to his unanswered phone call of some time earlier. He guessed that Benny C. wouldn't be answering any more calls for a while—if ever.

"I see." It was all the commissioner could manage at the moment.

"Here's the deal," La Mancha said briskly, not waiting for any questions. "Deliver the lady in good working order, and I'll give you an hour's head start before I start making calls."

Smalley saw red for an instant, his hands clenched into tight fists before him. He imagined the smell of something burning in his nostrils.

"You can't be serious!" he snapped, when he recovered himself enough to speak.

"Is that your answer?" La Mancha asked.

"What?"

Smalley was suddenly confused, his anger blunted, thrown off stride by the simple question.

La Mancha's voice came back at him, this time with a note of resignation in it.

"Goodbye, Commissioner."

Suddenly desperate, Smalley clutched at the desk-top speaker with palsied hands, as if to forcibly stop the other man from hanging up.

"Wait, dammit!" he blurted. Then he felt, tickling the back of his mind, the germ of an idea. "All right," he said reluctantly, "you've got a deal."

"Where and when?"

And suddenly Smalley knew the answer. Hell, he knew *all* the answers.

"You know Phalen Park?" he asked slowly, fighting to keep the new excitement out of his voice.

"I'll find it," La Mancha told him.

"Okay. Meet me on West Shore Drive, let's say in an hour."

There was no immediate answer, and Smalley assumed the guy was thinking it over.

"Safe and sound, Commissioner," La Mancha said at last. "Otherwise, all bets are off."

"How do I know I can trust you?" Smalley countered.

"What choice do you have?" the stranger asked simply.

Roger Smalley had no ready answer for that one, but it didn't matter, because the line was already dead, an obnoxious dial tone filling the room until he hit the speaker switch and silenced it.

The assistant commissioner sat quietly, thinking and cursing to himself, laying the last of his battle plans that warm morning. This La Mancha, whoever the hell he was, appeared to have him by the balls, and it wasn't a comfortable feeling.

Well, let the bastard think that way. Just let him.

Roger Smalley wasn't done yet. Not by a long shot. And Mr. Smart-ass La Mancha would wind up wearing his own balls for a bow tie before the afternoon was out.

You could take that to the bank.

La Mancha had gained the early advantage in their conversation via the element of surprise, but the shoe was on the other foot now. When the guy kept their appointment in the park, he would meet with a surprise arranged by Assistant Police Commissioner Roger Smalley, no less. A fatal surprise.

Smalley lifted the telephone receiver, thought better of it, then cradled it again.

No, it wasn't likely that his phones were tapped, or his office bugged, but he hadn't survived this long on the force with the wise guys on one side and the headhunters from Internal Affairs on the other by being careless.

It might be a sign of paranoia, but what the hell. These were paranoid times he lived in, after all. A grin crossed Smalley's face as he thought of a psychedelic poster that had seen brief popularity in the head shops a number of years earlier: "Just because you're paranoid, it doesn't mean they aren't out to get you!"

And amen to that.

Well, "they" could be surprised right alongside Mr. La Mancha.

Smalley rose from his desk and made ready to leave the office. He had plans to finalize and a surprise party to orchestrate. When it was over, he just might come back and take his attractive secretary out to lunch.

In an hour he would be home free. Free and clear.

18

The automobile bearing Fran Traynor, blindfolded, to her unknown destination slid smoothly to a stop. Throughout the ride, of which she remembered very little, she had been primarily conscious of the throbbing pain in her skull where Smalley had struck her, and of the moist, threatening palm that rested heavily on her right thigh.

But now the car had stopped, and the hot hand was withdrawn. She felt cool air upon her face as the doors opened on both sides, and the seat lurched as her unseen companions exited. Immediately, a hand was groping for her, fingertips trailing deliberately across the curve of one breast before locking onto her arm in a painful grip. Fran tried to pull away from that imprisoning hand, but there was nowhere to go, no place to hide.

She let herself be pulled from the car and led along a concrete drive, then over grass to another walkway.

"This way, babe," a male voice prodded from her left. "Watch your step."

She felt gingerly ahead of her with one foot, locating steps and taking them carefully, one at a time. She both heard and felt a door open in front of her, and then she was propelled through it, into the cool interior of a building. From the sounds and smells of the place, and the carpeting beneath her feet, she knew she was inside a house.

There were hands on both her arms now, guiding her left and right through what felt like a maze of corridors. Fran was becoming disoriented, cursing silently to herself as she realized that in her present condition, a simple living room filled with furniture could be made to feel like a winding labyrinth.

She recognized the feeling of a corridor, and had begun to count her paces when the guiding hands suddenly brought her up short, turning her sharply to the left. Keys rattled in a lock, and another door was opened for her, another hand shoving her inside.

Behind her head, blunt fingers tugged at the knot of her blindfold, and suddenly it came free, whisking across her face and disappearing behind her.

"Sit tight, doll," the leering voice said. "Maybe we can have some laughs later."

Fran half turned toward that voice, but the plain wooden door was already snapping closed, keys grating in the lock outside.

She stood there for a long moment, blinking her eyes to regain her full sense of sight. The room was dimly lit by a bare bulb overhead and was apparently without windows or other access to the world outside.

"Fran? Is that you?"

The lady cop whirled around, shocked by the

sound of a familiar female voice close behind her. She was surprised to see the face of Toni Blancanales regarding her from a corner of the room.

The girl crossed quickly to her, taking one of Fran's cold hands in both of hers.

"Toni!" the lady cop blurted. "What are you doing here?"

Toni was red-eyed from crying, her face pale, hair disheveled.

"Some men came to my apartment," she began haltingly. "They had guns, and . . . and . . . ."

The girl broke off, trembling slightly, and Fran slid a comforting arm around her slender shoulders, leading her back to the small couch that was the room's only furniture.

"Did they hurt you?" Fran asked, dreading the answer.

Toni looked up at her through tear-filled eyes, reading the implicit meaning of the officer's words.

"No, not the way you mean," she said, watching the relief flood into Fran's face. "They roughed me up a little. I fought them."

Fran looked closer now, and yes, she could make out a purple bruise along the curve of Toni's left cheek.

"Good," she said through gritted teeth.

"What's this all about, Fran?"

Fran Traynor hardly knew where to begin.

"It's a long story," she said at last, "and I don't have all of it yet. It's hard to believe."

"We're in danger, Fran," Toni said somberly. "I can feel it."

The lady cop nodded grimly. "I think we can expect the worst. If we get a chance to run, I say we take it."

Toni Blancanales seemed less frightened and shaky now that she was no longer alone.

"I have an idea why I'm here, Fran," she said softly. "But how did they get you? Why?"

Fran took a deep breath, and began relating the story of the morning's events, up through the disastrous meeting with Assistant Commissioner Smalley outside Calvary Cemetery. She left nothing out. For an instant she thought Toni brightened at the mention of the big fed, La Mancha, but the moment passed instantly, and Fran wrote it off as imagination resulting from stress.

"It was Smalley running interference all along," she said, summing up. "Probably with Jack Fawcett. I owe you one hell of an apology for being so blind, Toni."

Toni took her hand, no longer cold, and squeezed it tightly.

"Don't be silly," she said. "It isn't your fault at all. We're in this together."

And so they were.

The two women sat quietly together for several moments, discussing tentative escape plans in hushed tones, rejecting each in turn as too risky or too impractical. The interior of the room, as Fran had first thought, was windowless, with only the single door for entrance and exit. Aside from the moth-eaten sofa, the bare bulb overhead, and a few dated magazines scattered in one corner, the room and its adjoining bathroom had been expertly stripped of anything that might be converted for use as a weapon.

They were alone and unarmed, yes, and apparently defenseless.

While they were talking, a telephone jangled somewhere, several rooms away by the sound, and was quickly answered. Moments later, the women fell silent as heavy footsteps approached along the corridor outside.

The door swung inward to admit a hulking man in dark suit and sunglasses, a black .45 automatic held casually in his massive right hand. Behind him, other bodies blocked out the light from the corridor.

When the gunman spoke, Fran instantly recognized the voice of the gorilla who had fondled her thigh in the car.

"Time to go for a ride, ladies," he said, leering, and pausing for a wink at Fran. "Looks like we won't have time for laughs after all."

Fran took a look at the barrel of the .45, then glanced at Toni and back again at the gunman's eyes, invisible behind his shades.

And suddenly she wondered if there was any time left at all.

Mack Bolan pulled his sedan up beside Pol Blancanales's car in the shopping center parking lot. Pol left his car quickly and climbed in on the passenger side of Bolan's.

The Executioner saw in his old friend's face the same tautness, the same reckless, uncaring anger that he had seen so often on other faces on the eve of battle.

"Let's roll, buddy," the Politician snapped, rubbing his hands nervously together.

Bolan's voice was low, cautious as he answered.

"Easy, Pol. We can't afford to blunder in and mess things up for Toni."

Pol thought about that for a moment, then nodded grimly.

"You're right. As usual."

"What can you tell me about Phalen Park?" the Executioner asked his friend, putting the car in motion as he spoke.

Pol was quiet, thinking. Then he began speaking in the tone of a lecturer.

"It's on the north side of town," he began. "Part of it runs over into Maplewood there. It's got a lake...Phalen Lake, naturally. I guess the park gets its name from the lake, or vice versa."

"What about the terrain?" Bolan prodded.

Pol shrugged.

"Most of the southern half is a golf course, I think. North of the line and all along the water you've got trees and things. You know...a park."

Bolan could sympathize with Pol's obvious impatience, sure, but grim experience had taught him that a knowledge of apparent trivia could decide the outcome of a battle. And a battle could very well decide the outcome of a war, damned right.

Bolan was trying to visualize the layout of the park when Pol's voice intruded.

"Listen, what's the action, Sarge? How do we get Toni back in one piece?"

"Well, Smalley chose the meeting place," Bolan said at last, "and given his track record, we've got to anticipate a suck play. We go in ready for anything and see what develops. Play the ear."

"I still can't believe it," Pol said, sounding slightly shell-shocked. "The goddamned *commissioner.*"

His voice was heavy with a mixture of anger and disgust.

"It happens," Bolan told him softly. "We can let someone else sort out the details when Toni's safe and sound."

Pol's answer was a snarl coming at him through clenched teeth.

"If he's hurt her, Mack...I swear, if anyone's hurt her again...."

He bit the sentence off, leaving it unfinished.

"Easy, Pol. Don't borrow grief."

Blancanales shook his head grimly.

"I've had it, that's all. If she's not all right... just don't try to get in my way, buddy."

Bolan was disturbed by his friend's anger, even though he understood it perfectly. The Executioner had always lived by a set of simple, self-imposed rules. And one of those, carved in granite, was that he would never—repeat, never—fire upon a cop.

Good, bad, or indifferent, no matter how venal

or vicious a particular officer might prove to be upon examination, all of them were—or at least once had been—soldiers on the same side of the endless war against rampaging Animal Man. The cops stood for something, yeah, and Bolan hated the thought of drawing a bead on that symbol of law and order.

Still, he told himself, there was Toni...and Pol. If they were entering a trap, and Toni was injured or worse, how would he himself react?

Would he have the strength to stay his wrath and let slower justice take its winding course?

Would he try to hold back the angry, grieving man at his side?

And how far do you go to protect a tarnished soldier of the same side when he's proven guilty of murder, and worse? Do you turn a weapon on your friend to save a traitor?

Mack Bolan cursed silently to himself, knowing there was no way in the world to answer any of these crucial questions in advance.

They crossed St. Paul in good time, heading northeast on East Seventh to Arcade Avenue, then north to the intersection of Maryland Avenue. That took them west to meet West Shore Drive at the foot of Phalen Park, and there Bolan slid his rental car to a halt beneath a copse of roadside trees.

He checked his watch and found that they were slightly more than five minutes ahead of Roger Smalley's timetable.

So much the better. They would have time to lay some tentative plans.

Bolan reached into the back seat and pulled forward his flight bag filled with clanking armament.

"Let's suit up," he said simply, his eyes locking briefly with Pol's.

Blancanales nodded agreement, reaching into the flight bag to check through the arms sequestered there, selecting a portable assortment of lethal hardware for himself.

"Even when you travel light, you come prepared," he said to Bolan, forcing a grin that he obviously didn't feel.

Bolan answered with a cold smile of his own.

"Name of the game, buddy."

And as they sorted out their arms and ammunition, Mack Bolan began to speak rapidly, outlining a plan of action with alternate contingencies, knowing all the while that the lives of Toni, Pol, and himself were resting on his words.

They would, all of them, be tested in fire soon enough.

19

The sleek black crew wagon sat on the grassy shoulder of West Shore Drive, facing north. Away to the right, or east, Lake Phalen was hidden from view behind a sheltering screen of trees and shrubbery.

Riding shotgun in the front, crew chief Danny Toppacardi was getting nervous. He checked his watch at frequent intervals, mentally marking off the minutes until their scheduled rendezvous with the man. He wasn't late—not yet—but Danny Tops was already feeling the strain.

Not that the other members of the crew seemed put out by the waiting. In the driver's seat beside him, Lou Nova was working his way through his third cigar of the morning, puffing contentedly away. In the back, gunners Vince Cella and Solly Giuffre had the broads sandwiched in, and they weren't feeling the sweat, no way. Solly kept one arm looped around the lady cop's shoulders, and the fingers of his free hand were tracing little abstract patterns on her knee.

Danny heard a slap from back there, and the lady cop was saying, "Stop that!" in a no-nonsense tone. The crew chief turned around in time to see her straightening her skirt and Solly pulling back his hand like a kid caught reaching into the cookie jar.

The gunner flashed him a vacuous, shit-eating grin, and said, "No sweat, Danny. We're A-okay back here, right, momma?"

The policewoman just glared at him silently.

Perfect, just perfect. Danny felt disgust rising in him, on top of the nerves.

"Cool it, Solly," he drawled. "This ain't no social outing."

Chastised, the gunner lost his smile, replacing it with a petulant expression.

"Sure, Danny," he groused. "Whatever."

Toppacardi turned back toward the front, staring at nothing through the Lincoln's broad windshield. Sure, he could understand and sympathize with the restlessness of his troops. They had been on station for fifteen minutes, waiting for Old Man Smalley to grace them with his presence and take the two broads off their hands. That was a long time to spend sitting out in broad daylight with two kidnapped women in the back seat. Too damn long, yeah.

Hell, Danny could feel the restiveness himself, even if he couldn't afford to let it show.

Fifteen minutes sitting in the park with nothing to look at but trees and birds, and one car that had cruised by a few minutes earlier, putting everybody on edge. No wonder Solly and Vince were feeling their oats back there with the broads.

Danny wouldn't have minded cutting a slice of that for himself, but a job was a job, dammit. The boys should keep that in mind.

Another two minutes had passed, and Danny Toppacardi had checked his watch twice more before Roger Smalley's car pulled up and slid to a stop on the grassy shoulder ahead of them. The old man got out and walked back to meet them, his face locked into one of those politician's smiles that Danny Tops had learned to distrust on sight.

And Smalley took his own damn time about reaching the side of the car, finally getting there and leaning in through the window with his arms crossed on the sill, grinning at the broads in back.

"Ladies, I trust your accommodations were adequate," he said politely,

And the lady cop snapped back, "Go to hell, Smalley!"

Danny watched the old guy's face, stifling a grin that tugged at the corners of his mouth. He liked nothing better than to see a pompous ass deflated, but the dude was a paying customer, and he couldn't forget that either.

The crew chief's face was blank, impassive, as the assistant commissioner turned to address him for the first time.

"Any problems?" Smalley asked.

Danny Tops gave his head a casual shake.

"Nothin' we couldn't handle," he said. "What do you want us to do with the load?"

Smalley tossed another quick glance back toward the women.

"I should be taking them off your hands momentarily," he said.

As if on cue, another car rolled past them, easing to a stop some yards ahead of Smalley's vehicle. It bore no markings, but the four hardmen made it instantly as a police cruiser. They tensed reflexively, hands starting the casual slide toward hidden guns. Roger Smalley noted the reaction and tried to calm them with reassuring words.

"Relax," the commissioner said, "he's with me. There's no problem."

Danny Tops kept his hand inside his jacket, just in case. He watched a husky cop in plainclothes exit the cruiser and walk around to pull a skinny, pasty-faced kid from the passenger's side. The kid looked twenty-one, twenty-two tops. His hands were cuffed behind him, and his darting eyes had the desperate look of a cornered animal.

Roger Smalley was grinning like a shark with prey in sight.

"I believe we're all ready now. If one of you gentlemen could help me escort the ladies to the lake. . . ."

"That's me," Vinnie called from the back seat, already crawling out and reaching for the broad nearest him.

Danny glanced back in time to catch Solly scowling at the other gunner, and Vince Cella was waggling an upraised middle finger at him, snickering derisively.

"Maybe next time, Solly," he said, playing it to

the hilt. Solly Giuffre's answer was a husky growl.

Commissioner Smalley stepped back to make room as the two broads were half carried, half pulled out of the back seat. In another moment they were on the shoulder of the road, with Vince holding each one by an arm, grinning broadly.

"Excellent," the commissioner said, turning to Danny. "There is one other thing. I'm expecting some, er, unwelcome company. A man, probably alone. When he arrives, make him comfortable until I get back. Understood?"

"Yeah, yeah. Sure."

And that was all Danny Toppacardi needed on that sunny summer morning. First he brings his crew out to the park, where they park in broad daylight for a quarter-hour with two hot broads in the back, and now he's waiting for some wild card to appear from who knows where. And all the time they're sitting there, Vince and the two cops are off at the lake doing God knows what to the two broads.

He shook his head wearily, letting his breath out slowly in a long, disgusted sigh.

At age forty, he could remember the good old days when cops were bought off or frightened off or rubbed out. None of this kowtowing bullshit in those days, no sir. It wasn't right, somehow. He could feel it in his bones.

Danny watched as the little group disappeared into the trees and underbrush, Smalley leading the way like some kind of movie star with his entourage. Vinnie Cella went next, with the broads held close on either side of him, and the husky detective brought up the rear, keeping a tight watch on the scrawny kid. In a moment they were all lost to sight, leaving Danny Tops alone with his crewmen and his thoughts.

They settled down to wait, Danny firing up a smoke and passing the pack to Solly in the back seat. Still sulking, the gunner waved him off.

Maybe a minute after Smalley and his group had faded into the trees, a tall man in Windbreaker and slacks appeared up ahead of the Lincoln, walking along on the opposite side of the drive at a casual pace, his nose buried in the morning newspaper.

Danny and Lou Nova saw him at the same time, and the wheelman came erect in his seat, growling, "We got company."

From the back seat, Solly Giuffre chimed in, "Back here, too, Danny."

The crew chief craned his neck and caught sight of a second, smaller man, togged out in sweat clothes and jogging in the opposite direction along the far side of the drive. As he sat there watching, the two men closed on a collision course, the jogger puffing and watching his feet, while the big guy was lost in his paper.

And damned if they didn't collide, right out there with nothing but wide open space all around, jostling each other off stride with the impact.

The wheelman chuckled gleefully. "Stupid bastards."

Danny let himself relax, his hand sliding free of his jacket again.

The big man was looking around himself as if in a daze, the rumpled newspaper dangling from limp hands. And the little jogger was bent over double, clutching his side, all red in the face from his wheezing and puffing. The little guy's mouth started working, and Danny could tell he was chewing the big lummox up one side and down the other, damning him for a clumsy ass.

The big guy stood there taking it for several seconds, his reticence making the little man bolder. The jogger stepped closer, pushing his reddened face up at the big man's like a baseball player giving hell to the umpire on TV. The big guy was trying to answer, but he couldn't seem to get a word in edgewise.

Suddenly, the jogger snatched the papers from the big guy's hand and threw them down on the ground, going into a little dance step on top of them, grinding them into the turf with his sneakers.

Lou and Solly were laughing openly now, and Danny couldn't suppress the grin that worked at his mouth any longer, watching the comic spectacle.

"Christ, it's better than television," he said to no one in particular.

Growing bolder by the moment, the little guy reached up and slapped his large opponent hard across the face, back and forth, making his head rock from the sudden impact of the blows. Danny saw the color flood into his cheeks as something snapped inside, and instantly the two men were grappling madly in a clench, arms flailing, legs twisting and twining as they fought without any thought of timing or strategy.

"I got ten on the little fart," Solly called from the rear.

"You're covered, slick," Lou snapped, keeping his eyes on the action across the street.

Danny Tops watched, amused, as the two combatants staggered and grappled their way into the middle of West Shore Drive. Their diagonal course was bringing them toward the crew wagon, and after a moment Danny noted with surprise that they were almost on top of the Lincoln, moving with surprising speed as they fought.

The crew chief's smile slipped a notch, but he was caught up in the action now, ignoring the little alarm bell that sounded in the back of his mind.

Suddenly, the two men were at the car, butting against the fender, still flailing at each other and cursing a blue streak. The little guy wriggled free long enough to land a looping right on the big man's cheek, wringing a whoop of vicarious support from Solly in the back seat.

Purple with rage, the big man grabbed his wiry opponent under the armpits, taking another flurry of blows in the process, and hurled him bodily over the hood of the Lincoln. The little guy hit once on the way over, emitting a short squawk, and then disappeared over the far edge of the fender.

Danny Tops was suddenly angry. Worse, he smelled a rat.

"Now wait a fucking minute!" he growled, flinging open his door. He was halfway out of the car when the little guy reappeared, crouching beside the fender, a squat automatic pistol with silencer leveled in a two-handed grip.

The crew chief's mouth dropped open, and he felt his bowels loosening. After a split second he started to reach for his own weapon, and the little guy shot him, twice, calm as you please.

Pop-pop!

Danny Toppacardi sat down hard, the hot pain in his abdomen merging at once into icy cold and numbness from the armpits down. He couldn't reach his holstered .38, or even change positions as he sat there. It was as if his voluntary muscles had suddenly ceased to function.

Off to his left, he heard cursing from Lou and Solly, followed at once by more popping noises and the sound of breaking glass. Beside him in the front seat, Lou Nova was jerking and writhing under the impact of high-velocity slugs. A strangled yelp, quickly extinguished, was all he heard from Solly Giuffre in the back seat.

Danny felt a warm wetness in his lap and looked down, seeking its source. He was surprised to find himself sitting in a swamp of blood, much of it his, and all mixed up in a mass of pulpy tissue that looked suspiciously like brain matter.

Jesus! Lou's brains?

The door sprang open beside him, and suddenly

the little jogger had a pistol thrust in Danny's face, his free hand gripping the crew chief's shoulder tightly. His lips were moving quickly, but the sounds seemed somehow delayed on their way to Danny Toppacardi's ears.

"Where are they?" he heard at last. "Smalley and the girl, where'd they go?"

Danny's head lolled limply on his shoulder. He tried to answer, but the words came out sounding like "mmpf loggly." He felt something warm and wet overflowing his lips, coursing down his chin.

"Come on, dammit!" the little guy was shouting, shaking him roughly so that something rattled and snapped inside of him. "*Where are they?*"

Danny was staring past the florid, twisted face of his tormentor, toward the hazy screen of trees thirty yards off. He could almost imagine the lake beyond, a breeze making ripples on the surface of the water.

It would be nice to slip beneath that surface and just float away.

Somewhere behind Danny Tops and to his left, a deeper voice was coming through the fog, saying, "Come on, Pol. The lake."

Yeah, the lake, right.

And the two guys were sprinting away from the Lincoln, leaving Danny Toppacardi sitting there in a pool of blood. He watched them go, jogging across the emerald grass, their movements merging into slow motion as they reached the screen of undergrowth and plowed on through, fading from sight.

Danny Tops watched them disappear, wishing he could follow. When they were gone, he sat alone in the vehicle of death, watching the sunlight fade from gold to crimson, sinking slowly into midnight black.

20

Roger Smalley stood on the shore of Lake Phalen, looking out across the calm, unruffled water. As far as he could see in each direction, north and south, there was no sign of life. The strollers and boaters would not appear until later in the morning, and by then he would be gone, his business finished.

He turned his back on the water to face the five persons arrayed before him. To his left, Jack Fawcett stood close beside a nervous-looking Courtney Gilman. On the right, hulking Vince Cella kept a tight grip and wary eye on his two female captives.

"We don't have much time," Smalley said, breaking the silence. "Let's get this over with."

In one smooth motion, he drew the snub-nosed .38 revolver from under his jacket and took two quick steps toward Fawcett and his prisoner. Before the detective could grasp what was happening, Smalley raised his weapon and fired a single shot into Courtney Gilman's scrawny chest. The dying boy sprawled on the grass, twitching briefly, and then lay still.

Jack Fawcett was visibly stunned. His jaw

worked silently for an instant before he found his voice.

"What the hell?" It was the best he could manage.

"It's simple," the commissioner told him. "You finally got a hot tip on that sex killer you've been tracking, and you rushed right over to make the collar. Unfortunately, you were too late to save his latest victims, but you were able to settle the score."

Smalley smiled coldly at Fawcett's vacant expression.

"You're a hero, Lieutenant," he finished happily.

The detective shook his head as if to clear it, forcing his words out one at a time.

"This is crazy...I mean, you can't get away with something like this."

Smalley kept the frozen smile in place.

"I'm not even here, Jack. And I assure you, we *will* get away with it. We have to."

Fawcett looked from his superior to the female captives and back again, the full import of Smalley's words finally coming through to him.

"You mean to kill them, too," he said numbly. It didn't sound like a question.

"What would you suggest, Jack?" Smalley asked, his voice dripping with sarcasm. "Perhaps a press conference, for them to tell their story nationwide?"

Fawcett looked bewildered, thinking fast but coming up empty.

"There has to be another way."

Smalley lost his smile then, and his answering voice cracked across the intervening distance like a whiplash.

"Let's hear it, Lieutenant," he snapped. "You've got thirty seconds."

Jack Fawcett looked angry and confused. Roger Smalley could almost see the gears turning behind his eyes, and he knew from the man's expression that he had no alternative suggestions.

The lieutenant glanced down at the dead boy beside him and finally turned away, shaking his head disgustedly.

"I want no part of this," he said, his voice almost a whisper.

Smalley's brusque laughter was a bitter rebuke.

"Too late to weasel out, Jack," he sneered. "But don't worry, you won't have to dirty your hands."

The commissioner turned toward Vince Cella and the women, his gun held steady on a level with his waist. When next he spoke, he was addressing himself to the leering gunman.

"What we need here is a crime of passion," he said simply. "Are you up to it?"

Vince Cella grinned wickedly, glancing from one of his prisoners to the other.

"Mister," he drawled, "I'm always up."

Toni and Fran chose that moment to make their break in opposite directions, but the hardman held them easily in place. Making a split-second decision, he cut Toni's legs from under her with one sweep of his ankle, cuffing her hard across the back of the head as she fell. She hit the ground and lay still, barely conscious.

Vince Cella turned his full attention toward the lady cop, releasing his grip on her arm to tangle his fingers in her hair, pulling her close to him. With her arms pinned securely, she could only twist and kick out ineffectually at his shins. The big man easily avoided the blows, his free hand pawing at the front of her blouse.

"C'mon, momma," he leered, "it's party time."

Roger Smalley looked on dispassionately, loosely covering all three of them with the .38 in his hand. A smile very much like a grimace was locked onto his face.

Mack Bolan and Pol Blancanales heard the shot that killed Courtney Gilman. They were in visual contact with their targets by the time Vinnie Cella slammed Toni to the ground and turned on Fran Traynor.

With one thrust of his powerful arms, the gunman hurled her to the ground. He stood over her, legs wide apart, hands busy with the buckle of his belt.

The warriors let him loosen it before they stepped out of concealment. Their silenced weapons scanned the killing ground, the sweeps including the hardman, Roger Smalley, and Jack Fawcett simultaneously.

Four faces turned to gape at the new, unexpected arrivals. The three men registered shock, but Fran Traynor's expression was tempered with heartfelt relief.

The Executioner addressed himself to Vinnie Cella.

"Careful, your pants could fall down."

"Funny man," the punk answered, trying to sneer and missing it by a mile.

Roger Smalley's voice demanded Bolan's attention.

"Ah, Mr. La Mancha, I presume?"

The commissioner held his gun leveled and ready to fire, the muzzle directed at some arbitrary midpoint between Bolan and the Politician.

Fawcett's voice answered for Bolan.

"That's La Mancha," the lieutenant said, pointing. "His partner's the brother."

Smalley wore a little quizzical smile.

"Of course, family loyalty," he said. "How touching. I must say I'm impressed. How did you get past. . . ."

He left it unfinished, his .38 waggling in the general direction of the invisible Lincoln and its cargo of death.

"They're out of it, Smalley," the Executioner told him. "It's down to you."

And the assistant commissioner's face was going through some changes, yeah, screwing itself up all at once into a mask of fury. It pleased Mack Bolan to see the older man lose his self-confident smile.

Across from Smalley, the gunsel was holding his loose slacks with one hand, clenching and opening the other convulsively. He was grinding his teeth in anger, his face livid.

"Danny, Lou, Solly...." he began, almost groaning. "You wasted 'em!"

Smalley saw his opening, tensing as he shouted, "Take them, dammit!"

Suddenly the scene erupted into frenzied action. Vince Cella was clawing for his holstered pistol with both hands, taking a backward step and stumbling as his suddenly unfettered slacks dropped down around his ankles. He started to fall, his weapon still hidden, and Bolan helped him get there with a single 9mm mangler through the bridge of his nose.

Roger Smalley was diving toward Toni's prostrate form. Pol saw the move and reacted, but a half-second too slowly. Before he could squeeze off a shot, the commissioner was into a crouch, clutching Toni in front of him in a sitting position, his .38 jammed against her temple.

"Easy, brother," he said, breathing heavily. "It's all over."

"Not yet, Commissioner."

Bolan's voice hit Smalley like a draft from the tomb, blanching the confidence from his face, but he made no move to lower the gun or release his hostage.

"I don't know who the hell you are," Smalley growled, "but you've blown it." He half turned to the detective, keeping his eyes firmly on Bolan and Pol. "Jack! Change of plans. We've got a gangland massacre on our hands. Use your weapon."

Behind Smalley, Jack Fawcett seemed to be moving in slow motion, drawing the .38 special from his belt and moving forward until he stood even with Smalley and the girl, perhaps ten feet to their right.

Mack Bolan read the hesitation on the lieutenant's face.

"Where does it stop, Smalley?" the Executioner called.

"It stops here, mister. Right here! All the loose ends tied up into one tidy knot, right around your neck."

Bolan forced a smile he didn't feel.

"With nine people massacred, one of them a police officer? Make sense, Commissioner."

"Shut up!" Smalley grated, turning again toward Jack Fawcett. "What are you waiting for? Kill them!"

Fawcett glanced from the two armed men to Smalley, and back again. He looked sick, desperate. The weapon in his hand was rising shakily.

"Jesus, Chief," he muttered, almost pleading.

Smalley was livid, his eyes snapping.

"Goddammit, you yellow bastard, I said use your weapon!"

The first shot hit Smalley in the right temple

and burst on through the other side in a shower of crimson. For an instant his face wore a frozen expression of shock, and then the second slug hit him, lifting the top of his skull and punching him over sideways in a lifeless sprawl.

Toni Blancanales, suddenly released from Smalley's death grip, toppled forward on her face.

Jack Fawcett stood over the commissioner's limp form and emptied his .38 into the bloody ruin of that face. Finally, when the hammer fell on empty chambers, he let the pistol tumble from slack fingers onto the bloody grass at his feet.

The detective turned toward Mack Bolan as Pol rushed to his sister's side. The face Bolan saw was that of a man turned suddenly old before his time.

"Your play, La Mancha," he said at last, hands spread in a gesture of surrender.

Bolan returned the Beretta to side leather, already moving to help Fran onto her feet.

"It's endgame, Jack," he said over his shoulder. "All bets are off. Every man for himself."

Jack Fawcett surveyed the scene of carnage around him.

"How the hell do I explain all this?" he wondered aloud. "Jesus, what a mess."

"How about the truth?" Bolan offered. "It's overdue."

The detective held his eyes for a long moment, then nodded wearily.

"Yeah," he sighed, "I guess."

Fran Traynor was dusting herself off and rubbing her bruised arms, watching Jack Fawcett all the while.

"There may be something I can do to help," she said. "I mean...I can explain about Smalley, at least."

"I appreciate that, Fran," Fawcett said, "but it's my mess. Nobody twisted my arm. I'll have to clean it up myself."

Pol Blancanales and his sister were already moving away from the killing ground. Toni was still shaky, and the Politician supported her with a strong arm around her shoulders.

Bolan started to follow them, then paused, turning back toward the two cops as they stood together, side by side.

"I'll drop a few words in the right places, Lieutenant," he said. "I can't gloss it over, but your help won't be forgotten, either."

Fawcett nodded grimly, making no move to stop the three of them as they faded into the trees.

Bolan moved quickly along behind Pol and Toni, watching them closely as they backtracked toward the waiting rental car. There was a sort of emptiness inside him, now that the play had unraveled, but another very important part of him felt full and warm.

It was over, for the moment, in St. Paul. A shadow of fear had been lifted from the Twin Cities. Some lives had been terminated, others changed irrevocably, but in the balance, Bolan felt good about the outcome of his unorthodox campaign.

And yeah, it was over at last. Watching Toni up ahead, the Executioner only hoped that the scars wouldn't linger too long.

EPILOGUE

Mack Bolan stood with Pol and Toni Blancanales, watching the sleek Lear jet taxi toward them through lowering dusk. He had been in St. Paul for less than twenty-four hours, but it had the feel of a long, grueling lifetime.

"You could use a rest," he said to both of them, including brother and sister in the sweep of his eyes. "Why don't you come back with me to the farm for a few days?"

Toni answered for them both.

"Thanks, maybe later," she said. "Right now, I really need to be alone and put the pieces back together."

Pol looked worried at that, but she laid a soft hand on his shoulder and smiled.

"I'm sorry, Rosario. There are some things a big brother just can't do for a girl."

The Politician lowered hurt eyes, nodding solemnly.

"Besides," Toni added, her voice suddenly upbeat, more animated than Bolan could remember hearing it that day, "I have to be around for the counseling sessions that Fran arranged before her transfer."

Pol and Bolan exchanged glances of pleasant surprise.

"They have a whole rape rehabilitation program here," the kid sister continued, sounding almost cheerful. Almost, but not quite.

"If the lady law is in charge, it sounds like a winner," Bolan said warmly.

Toni nodded. "You'll notice I can say it now. I was raped. So there. I have to come to terms with it before anybody else can, right?"

Bolan turned to Pol. "That's a hell of a lady you've got there," he said softly.

The Politician beamed. "Don't I know it."

"You're going to make it, Toni," Bolan said, holding her eyes with his own. "You've got the marks of a winner."

"Not the same played-out loser from this morning, eh?"

Her smile was infectious, and Bolan answered with one of his own.

Behind them, the engines of the Lear were winding up, the sleek fuselage catching the last rays of sun and reflecting them brilliantly.

The Executioner said his goodbyes, shaking hands warmly with Pol Blancanales. When he turned to Toni, she stepped into his arms willingly, holding him tightly for several seconds and kissing his cheek before she disengaged.

"Thanks, friend," she whispered in his ear.

Bolan held her eyes with his for a long moment,

then nodded silently and put that place behind him.

It was over, yeah, in St. Paul.

And it was, the Executioner suspected, both an end and a beginning.

CODE BLUE
FROM WHITE HOUSE 171405E
TO PHOENIX/STONYMAN
BT
BROGNOLA SENDS X TOPMAN REQUESTS YOUR
IMMEDIATE PERSONAL ATTENTION FOR
SUPERSENSITIVE HANDLING X IRREFUTABLE
SOURCES INDICATE PRESENCE WASHDC AREA CRACK
IRANIAN DEATH SQUAD TARGETED FOR
ASSASSINATION POLITICALLY SENSITIVE EXILED
EX-OFFICIAL IRANGOV NOW ENJOYING SOFT
SANCTUARY USGOV X SUBJECT ALERTED AND
PREPARING DEPARTURE CONUS TOMORROW DAWN BUT
HIGHLY VULNERABLE TO OVERNIGHT ATTACK AND
CONSIDERED IN GRAVE PERIL X OFFICIAL USGOV
INTERVENTION/INVOLVEMENT HIGHLY
UNDESIRABLE DUE SENSITIVE RELATIONS PRESENT
IRANGOV HOWEVER MORAL OBLIGATION DICTATES
ALL POSSIBLE COVERT PROTECTION THIS SUBJECT
X REQUEST YOU HANDLE PER YOUR SOP AND ADVISE
BACKUP REQUIREMENTS X CONFIRM RECEIPT AND
ACCEPTANCE THIS VOLMISS ALSO RENDEZVOUS
POINT/TIME FOR PERSBRIEF X TOPMAN PERSONAL
REQUEST
BT
EOM

```
CODE BLUE
FROM STONYMAN 171418E
TO BROGNOLA/WHITE HOUSE
BT
APRIL SENDS X RE 171405E X PHOENIX ACCEPTS X
RENDEZVOUS POINT DELTA 1800E SOP FOR
PERSBRIEF X WILL ADVISE BACKUP REQUIREMENTS
AT THAT TIME X STONYMAN CLEAR AND STANDINGBY
FULL SUPPORT ALL BASE CAPABILITIES X KEEP ME
INFORMED
BT
EOM
```

MACK BOLAN

THE EXECUTIONER 42

BOLAN

The Iranian Hit

Coming in May
from Gold Eagle Books

It was twilight, and Bolan was prowling the deserted streets of Potomac, an affluent Maryland suburb. Somewhere in these lush environs was hidden the secret of his latest mission. And then he saw her through his Starlight spotting scope. Blonde, attractive, leather-jacketed, alone. And with a look of terror on her face.

The woman was the American wife of an Iranian exile, General Eshan Nazarour. Former top officer of Savak, the Shah's secret police. He was marked for assassination by an Arab hit team. And the countdown for elimination had begun.

Bolan yanked the wheel of his Corvette to the right.

The sleek black sportscar left the road and went sailing up the side of the embankment. Railroad tracks cluttered underneath. The car overshot and was momentarily airborne. Then it crashed to rest in a four-point landing that shuddered through the chassis.

Bolan grabbed his Uzi and catapulted out from the Corvette's passenger side, his black garb molding him to the darkness.

He squeezed off a short burst at his ambushers, who were taking wild and useless aim at the black car in the night. It was enough to fell three men in a withering hail, stitched from left to right at upper chest level. The Uzi's muzzle illuminated the darkness in flashes.

Hardman number four had been pinning his female captive to the hood of a Malibu. Now he was straightening, forgetful of the blonde as he pawed for hardware beneath his jacket. The woman dashed from the man's side, losing herself in the night.

The heavy had his weapon halfway out when the Uzi burped again, almost discreetly. The force of the 9mm rounds smashed the man against the car. Then he pitched forward onto the grass alongside the road, his right hand still reaching under his left arm in a final statement of purpose.

The silence was all-enfolding. The car, the bodies—Bolan could see no sign of the lady. . . .

Cautiously, he approached.

Wondering just what the hell had gone down here.

Wondering about the whole goddam mission.

Wondering what would happen next.

Watch for The Iranian Hit, Executioner #42, wherever paperbacks are sold—May 1982.

Coming in June
from Gold Eagle

ABLE TEAM

AN EXECUTIONER SERIES

by Don Pendleton
and Dick Stivers

In Able Team #1: *Tower of Terror*, and Able Team #2: *The Hostaged Island*
Bolan's Death Squad is reborn at last

Carl Lyons, Pol Blancanales and Gadgets Schwarz are back. They are now a team, recruited by the big guy to tackle terrorist outrages too volatile and unpredictable for regular law enforcement.

Lyons, Blancanales and Schwarz confront a terrorist group that has hijacked an entire New York office building in *Tower of Terror*, and take on a vicious motorcycle gang that is holding Catalina to ransom in *The Hostaged Island*.

These are stories in the bestselling tradition of The Executioner, authored by the world's leading writer of heroic action adventure.

Watch for Able Team in the bookstores soon!